Whitney Louisa Goddard

Peasy's Childhood

Stories for Children, and for all who Remember that they have been Children

Whitney Louisa Goddard

Peasy's Childhood
Stories for Children, and for all who Remember that they have been Children

ISBN/EAN: 9783744751551

Printed in Europe, USA, Canada, Australia, Japan

Cover: Foto ©Andreas Hilbeck / pixelio.de

More available books at **www.hansebooks.com**

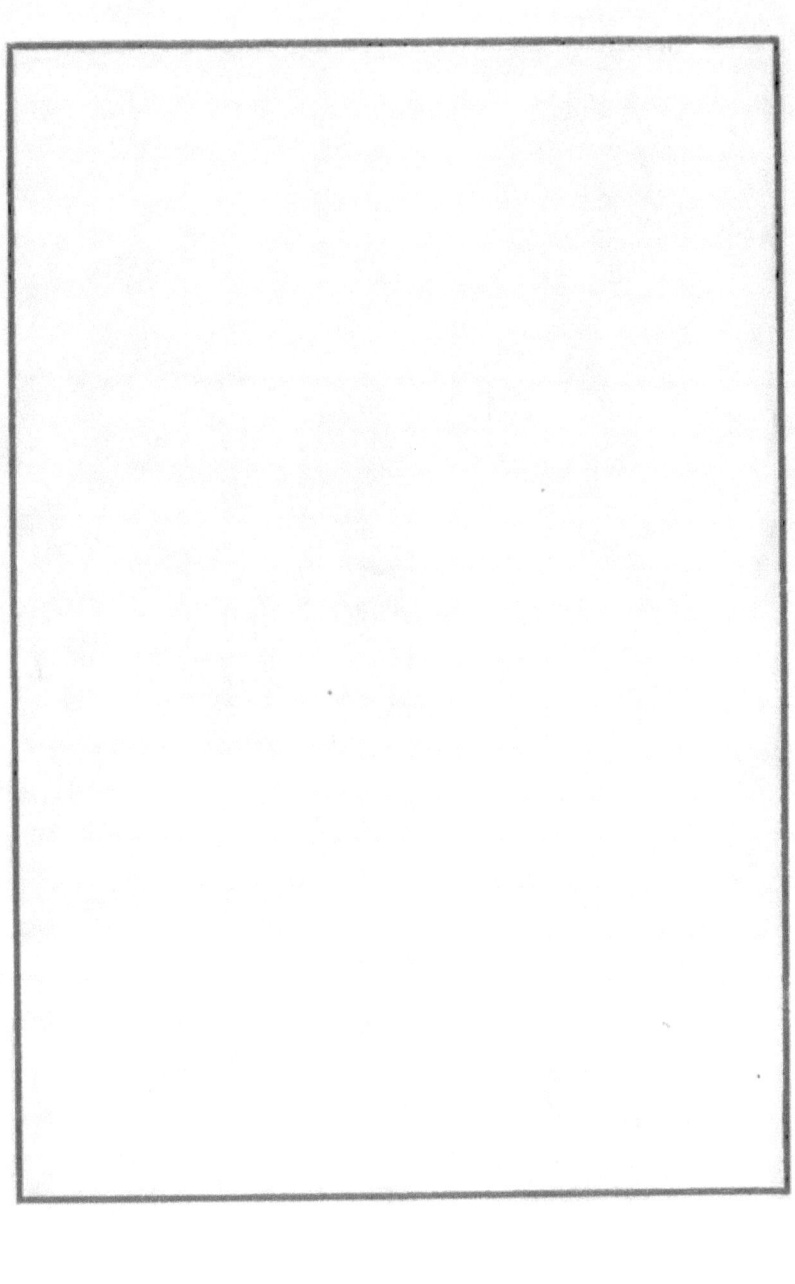

PEASY'S CHILDHOOD.

PEASY'S CHILDHOOD:

STORIES FOR CHILDREN,

AND FOR ALL WHO REMEMBER THAT THEY
HAVE BEEN CHILDREN.

CAMBRIDGE, MASS.
UNIVERSITY PRESS.
1878.

CONTENTS.

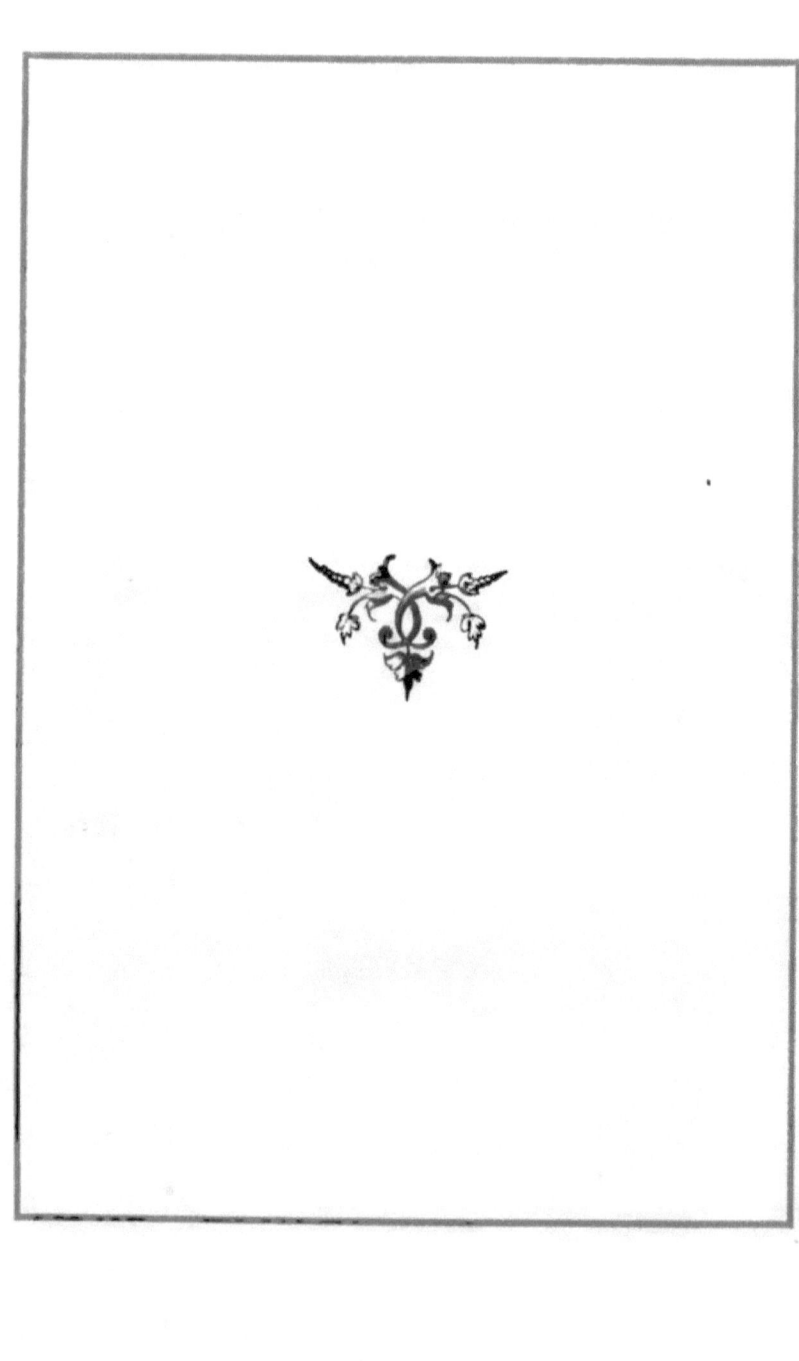

PEASY'S CHILDHOOD.

ONE summer afternoon, not very long ago, I
was standing upon the summit of the Rigi,
from whence on a clear day one of the finest views
in the world is to be seen. But this was *not* a clear
day, and strain my eyes as I would, nothing was
visible but the warm smiling blue sky above and the
cold gloomy ocean of mist below. From the top of
solitary Rockall in the midst of the Atlantic one
gets just about such a prospect; only on the Rigi
one is not surrounded by the nests and the fluttering
wings of sea-birds; Alpine roses and blue gentians
grow at one's feet instead; and the distant tinkling
of herd-bells soothes one's ear in place of the clangor
and screaming of gulls and mews.

So there I stood upon the mountain, half wondering, half disappointed, looking down into the mist. Suddenly it began to assume consistency, to be furrowed, to be heaped into ridges, to form hills and valleys, to be varied with lights and shadows. Then it looked like the pale ghost of the earth with all its heights and plains in winding-sheets. Soon it began to rock and reel, as if the ghost of an earthquake had taken possession of it, and under my very eyes a tremendous fissure opened. Ah, what did I see! A lake sparkled, meadows glowed in sunshine, white dots of villages nestled against dark forests, — it was all so distinct, yet so very far beneath me. I thought of the peasant in the story who peeped down between two sods and saw the very centre of the earth and all the glories of fairy-land. But almost before I had time for the thought the fissure closed, the vision vanished, and another appeared, even in the midst of my first sigh of disappointment. Yes, there they stood, those giants of the Bernese Oberland, glorifying the horizon like a company of archangels with their white wings folded.

And so, for a long time, the magical earthquake rocked and heaved and gave up its splendors. Just so it is with the remembrances of early childhood. The heavy mist of oblivion blots out most of the events of our first days, but here and there, we know not how or why, it parts, — and certain scenes, certain occurrences, certain periods even, stand out from among its dark folds in perfect distinctness of outline, and bathed in that wonderfully clear atmosphere which belongs only to these very early memories. This I thought to myself as I was descending the Rigi on the next day, amid singing torrents and dancing birches.

Then I began to have a desire to put into words some of these little enamelled pictures of my own childish memory, and after I had gratified this desire, I began to ask myself if there might not be other children who would like to get acquainted with *my* childhood. In writing these stories I seemed to grow young again and to long for playfellows of a new generation. Will you take me among you, dear little children?

I.

MY FIRST SCHOOL.

AFTER my sister Anne and I had left our dear English home to live in America we became " thorough little John Bulls," as people used to call us. William IV. was king of England then, the predecessor of Queen Victoria, and we professed the greatest loyalty to him. We knew the names of the royal dukes, his brothers, and their children, the names of the English nobility, and their country-seats, and the titles of their eldest sons, all of which we studied out of certain pamphlets in our father's possession. We adored everything English and despised everything American, and we had daily quarrels with our schoolfellows on that account. We could boast of Lord Nelson and the Duke of Wellington, while they declared that General

Washington and Lafayette were a great deal "smarter men." They would whistle " Yankee Doodle," while we sang " God save the King" at the top of our lungs, each party trying to make more noise than the other. Our mother rather sympathized with us in our British loyalty, which made us very proud, but we thought she fell away from grace terribly, when we saw her eating squash and sweet corn with relish, and declaring she liked them. *We* never tasted them, nor Indian puddings, nor brown bread, nor baked beans, for these articles of food were unknown in England, and we professed to shudder with disgust when they were offered to us. " Which do you like best, treacle or molasses?" people would ask us, and with one voice we answered "Treacle," which is the English word for molasses; but we did not know that. We thought English ways and English people were perfect, and we were so sensitive on that point, that if a word was said by any one to the contrary, we would rush out of the room, burst into tears, and sob indignantly in each other's arms. Two foolish children indeed we were!

One day a gentleman who had just returned from England called on my mother to bring her the last news of her friends there. He was dressed rather peculiarly, and I remember he told my mother that his clothes had been made in London. Anne and I were sitting on a couple of footstools (we never said *cricket*, for that was an American word) at his feet, and we simultaneously laid our heads gently against his knees, feeling that the touch of those English-made garments was almost sacred. He was a kind old friend, and he smiled approvingly down upon us at this mark of affection, which he little thought was paid to his trousers rather than to himself. But soon he began to talk to our mother about the discomforts of travelling in England for an American, and especially the want of variety in the food. "Why, ma'am," said he, "in Paris you find a confectioner's shop at every corner, and there you can get all kinds of jellies, tarts, and *garters*" (he meant *gateaux*). "But in an English city, even in London, if you go into a pastry-cook's shop for a bit of luncheon, when you are tired with sight-seeing, they never give you anything but

10

buns and beer, buns and beer. If any one asks me for what productions England is famous, I say *buns and beer."*

The gentleman laughed as if he had said something very funny, but we were sadly disappointed in him; we thought his manner of speaking of *buns* highly disrespectful. Buns had been the one luxury of our lives, before we left England; mamma had used them as rewards of merit, so that they were associated in our minds with all the virtues. If we spelled successfully a column of "Words in Four Syllables," standing with toes turned out, and hands behind our backs, we were presented with buns; if we "ran" the heels of papa's socks strictly according to the rule, "take up one thread and leave three threads," buns rewarded us.

When the old gentleman had finished his visit, my sister and I stood at the window and watched him crossing the street daintily in his new London clothes. The streets were full of melting ice and snow, and a sticky black mud, which spoiled every garment that it touched, so that we thought of nothing else

11

but how to keep out of it when we took our walks abroad.

Suddenly we saw running round the corner of the street a little boy, who laughed and shouted and looked back continually, sometimes stopping to dance in a derisive way; and in a moment his mother followed, also running, but very much out of breath; her face was very red, and she was making frantic signs to the naughty boy to stop. He had evidently broken away from her, and she never could have caught him in the world had he not carelessly fallen into the gutter, right into the very blackest of the mud. She pounced upon him at once, and in a whirlwind of confusion they disappeared again round the corner, she scolding the little boy, shaking him, wiping him, cuffing his ears till his cap fell over his eyes, and then cuffing it back again to its place, and he roaring at the top of his lungs, and promising to be a good boy, sputtering with his mouth full of mud.

"There is no such nasty mud as that in England," said I emphatically. "O, Anne, do you remember the lovely clean mud in Mr. Mason's back lane, where we used to keep a baker's shop and set out our mud cakes and rolls on the broken kitchen chair? Don't 'sturb me. I'm going into the corner to remember it all up." So down I sat behind the sofa, covering my eyes with my apron, and letting myself go back into my short past.

Yes, the first thing I ever made in my life was a dirt-pie. You may imagine how much I admired it when it was finished. The mud was just of the right consistency. I had shaped it with the crown of my hat, ornamented the edge with a row of white pebbles, and stuck bits of broken crockery all over the top in imitation of citron. " Ah," thought I, " if Anne would only come out and look at it, or even if nurse would bring the baby, *that* would be better than nothing." Unluckily my pie was erected in the very centre of the back lane, and I dared not leave it, even to run into the house for my little sister, lest some stray dog or cow should demolish it by walking through it. So I sat very patiently mounting guard in the middle of a deep rut, looking intently at the nursery-window, which just appeared over the

13

garden-hedge that bounded the lane, that I might beckon to little Anne the moment her face should show itself. But instead of Anne, my father was the first person who appeared, sauntering down the lane for an evening walk.

"O papa," cried I, as soon as he was near enough, "just look at my pie! Is n't it beautiful?"

I pointed to it proudly; I could not find any more words to express my admiration and satisfaction. They were too great for speech. But my father's face puzzled me a little; he did not look altogether enchanted.

"Beautiful? It's you who are beautiful," he cried; "you 're covered with dirt from head to foot. Yes, your hair is actually matted together with mud. Let 's see what your mother will say to you."

He took me up in his arms, and with one stroke of his foot he demolished all my handiwork. I burst into a loud roar of anger and mortification, a little consoled, however, by seeing that a piece of my citron had cut my father's boot sadly.

14

I did not get a very flattering reception in the house. My mother and the nurse looked at me with serious faces, making well-known sounds of disapprobation with their tongues against the roofs of their mouths. Even little Anne would not touch me when I held out to her a hand covered with black streaks and dirty tears.

"My dear," said my father to my mother, "how can you let this child get into such a state, and run about the neighborhood bareheaded like a young gypsy? It's very unsafe, very improper."

"My dear," replied my mother to my father, "what you say is very true; I thought she was safe and sound on the parlor-sofa with her picture-books; but with Anne and Lucretia and the baby to look after, I declare I cannot pay proper attention to Peasy. She must really be sent to school. Old Peggy Jones's daughter keeps a nice little school, and to-morrow morning I'll take Peasy down there without fail."

Next morning nurse brushed my hair till I was quite in a pet; a larger bib than usual was pinned

15

over my clean frock at breakfast, and I was charged not to spill my milk into my lap, " Because, miss, you are going to school." I had no idea what sort of place "school" was, but I did not like this air of preparation, nor did I like Peggy Jones, who often came to sew for my mother. I was sure, therefore, that I should not like her daughter.

After breakfast my hat was brought and tied under my chin. It had been washed and pressed to cleanse it from the fragments of dirt-pie, and the straw *creaked* very disagreeably. My mother took out of the closet a certain detestable primer, full of great staring A B C's. Often had I been called from the most delightful plays to stand at her knee, and follow the point of her pin down the long column of letters which adorned the first page. I did not like the primer, it was associated with too many gentle reminders of my mother's thimble on my stupid little head.

"You are to take this to school," said my mother, putting the book into a sombre green satchel.

"O no, mamma," cried I, eagerly. "I don't want

it. I'd a great deal rather carry the 'Sixteen Wonderful Old Women,' or ' Deborah Dent.'"

"Peasy," said my mother in a solemn voice, "you are going to school to *learn.*"

My heart sank at once, nor was I much comforted by seeing mamma put two figs and a bun into the satchel. I felt sure they would taste of the primer. I took an affecting farewell of little Anne. I was in the habit of regulating my feelings a good deal by what I imagined to be the expression of her face. This time it was a very grave face.

"Good by, Anne, good by," I half sobbed. "I'll let you play with my churn while I'm gone, and you may put pins into Callie's eyes, if you want to," — Callie being a calico doll.

Mamma could wait no longer, so away we went together under her great parasol.

It was a morning of mornings! The breeze had all the warmth of summer and the freshness of spring; the hedges were full of little birds, who bustled noisily under the leaves, or burst out upon us suddenly from among them, with loud snatches

17

of song. "No wonder," thought I; "they are not going to school!" There was a sort of holiday brilliancy in the sunshine, and all the tiny blades of grass were dancing together. The wild rose-bushes were covered with flowers, which stared at me like so many great eyes, just as if they knew where I was going. I felt very unhappy and very cross.

"Peasy," said mamma, in her amiable way, "would not you like to pick a few of these roses to give to your teacher?"

"No," said I, with more decision than politeness.

When we reached the door of Peggy Jones's cottage, a great buzzing and humming of voices from within announced that school was already begun. Mamma was obliged to knock several times with the handle of her parasol before she could be heard. Meantime my ill-temper seemed to be "running out of the heels of my boots," and I was seized, instead, with a terrible fear and timidity which made me tremble all over. My heart beat, and a dimness came over my eyes. I could hardly see Miss Jones

18

when she opened the door, but her head seemed to tower up to the very ceiling. Mamma said something to me about " being a good girl," and " waiting after school till I was sent for," and then walked away with her usual composure, as if nothing was the matter. I was too much frightened not to be perfectly passive, and in this state I was led into the school, and through rows of girls up to the very top of the room. I only remember that these girls appeared to me like young giantesses with eyes bigger than the dog-roses, and more staring.

After Miss Jones had left me seated upon a little cricket with my back against the wall, I began to recover myself and to look about me. Not being used to children older than myself, and knowing nothing about their occupations and amusements, I found plenty of things to wonder at. I was at first completely absorbed in the *patchwork*. I thought the long strips of gay-colored pieces dazzlingly beautiful, and the squares of calico covered with vines and sprigs my imagination converted into pictures of garden-beds adorned with flowers.

19

By and by I perceived that there were a great many primers in the room just like mine. This was a disagreeable discovery, and quite diverted my mind from the patchwork. Several girls were holding their primers close to their faces, and spelling out of their columns in loud whispers. They rocked themselves backwards and forwards as if they were in great pain. I pitied them from the bottom of my heart. Pretty soon the classes went up to recite. I noticed how they all stood in a line, with their heels together, toes turned out and hands behind them. They reminded me of the awkward squad of a certain regiment which I had often seen drilling at M...., and I thought Miss Jones put out the words to spell with the fierceness of a drill-sergeant. Worse than that, *she* too wore a thimble like mamma, and used it in the same way. Worst of all, one very dull girl was made to stand in the corner with her face to the wall, for inattention to that terrible primer. My terror returned at this spectacle. I felt that I should never have courage to go up and say my letters, without even the aid of a pin;

I knew that I should be deprived of sight and
speech as soon as I found myself placed at Miss
Jones's awful knee, and I was sure that, after well
exercising her thimble upon my head, she would end
by placing me too in another corner, and that the
whole school would despise me. Then I thought
of home and of Anne. It seemed to me that years
had passed since I had seen them, and that it would
be years before I should see them again. O that
my mother could only know what I felt! And
this thought of mamma overcame my fortitude. I
began to cry vehemently, with my pinafore covering
my face. This made some confusion in the school;
but Miss Jones must have been a judicious teacher, for instead of scolding me she gently told me
that she supposed I was tired, and that I might
go out in the yard and play with some kittens
which she had. She told one of the large girls to
take me and show me the way, and added that I
need not come in till I felt better. As I persisted
in keeping my head and face concealed in my pinafore, I was led blindfold out of school, and

the children laughed till my cheeks tingled with shame.

When I found myself alone with the kittens I cried more than ever. The old cat was very kind; she licked off my tears and purred in a motherly way, so I soon felt a little better, and even untied the strings of my shoes for the kittens to play with. After a good romp with them in the fresh air, I gathered courage enough to think about returning into school. I ventured back to the door and tapped gently. But the first class was going through the multiplication-table, and nobody heard me. My courage vanished just as my ill-temper had done in the morning, and I took a desperate resolution: I would go home. To be sure I did not know the way, and I had never walked in the roads alone; but I would try, — anything was better than the primer and the girls' eyes. So I started, running with all my speed. The faster I ran the more agitated I became. I fancied the whole school was behind me, chasing me, and Miss Jones, with her long legs and her thimble, gaining upon me at every

step. I don't know how I found my way back, but
I am sure I must have startled my mother when I
burst into her parlor. I had no hat, only one shoe,
and the other was minus a string. My face was on
fire with heat and excitement, my hair in a snarl,
my clothes tumbled, and my neck and arms adorned
with long scratches, bestowed by my friends the
kittens. Little Anne was the first object that I
sought. She was sitting at the window in a high-
chair, all dressed in white, her grave, composed face
as cool and fresh-looking as her frock. She was
eating strawberries out of a white plate, with her
feet carefully turned out on the step of the chair.
I can see, as well as if they were before me now,
the gilt buttons of her shoes, and her socks so nicely
smoothed over the ankles. I flew towards her, and
peace and calmness passed into my childish being
as I laid my hot face in her lap. She said not a
word, but patted me with her little soft hands, and
pushed a strawberry into my mouth.

Mamma must have concluded that I was too
young to go to school. At least she did not re-

prove me for running away, nor offer to take me there again. She sent for my hat, for which I was very glad, and for my primer, for which I was very sorry. But I had lost my taste for dirt-pies, and I suppose she thought that was quite as much as she could expect from two hours' schooling.

II.

THE POOR LITTLE BABY.

ONE morning I was having a fine play in the nursery with little Anne. We "made believe" that we were riding to America to see our relations. We placed two chairs side by side for a chaise, and two others, turned down, were our horses. These were harnessed with a variety of old tapes and strings, and a couple of our sashes made excellent reins. We had our two nightgowns rolled up for baggage, and a small basketful of stones and chips, which represented cakes and buns. Father had been reading to me the "Pilgrim's Progress," where Christiana, Mercy, and four hungry boys make the journey to the Eternal City with no other provisions than an occasional pomegranate and a few bunches of grapes. So when Anne suggested that we might eat up our cakes before we got to America, and that we ought to provide ourselves with some chickens and loaves of bread, I quoted John Bunyan to her, and she yielded to my superior learning. Of course we did not intend to take so long a journey without meeting with adventures, and we made ourselves plenty of them. Our chaise broke down, upset, its wheels came off, its floor fell through; our horses stumbled, reared, kicked, and plunged. We had an idea that there was water to be crossed somewhere on the road to America, so we occasionally got down upon the floor and swam a little. We were having a delightfully noisy time.

By and by the baby, who was lying in nurse's lap, stirred uneasily, and began to cough and choke and struggle. This was nothing new to us, for the poor little fellow, though only four months old, had been suffering with the whooping-cough for some weeks. But this was a very bad fit of strangling, and nurse looked at the baby with great concern as she raised him and tried to make him comfortable.

"Poor dear!" said nurse, shaking her head, "he

gets weaker and weaker every day, he'll never get over it, — he can't bear it much longer," added she, as the poor little exhausted sufferer sank back with closed eyes and purple lips, after the paroxysm was over.

"What will he do," said I, "when he can't bear it any longer?"

"God will take him," answered nurse, gravely.

"But, Mary," said I, "why couldn't God take one of us three girls instead? Don't girls make as good angels as boys? And mamma has only one boy."

"Lord sakes, miss!" said Mary, which was not a very satisfactory answer.

This was Saturday, and on Saturday evening it was my mother's custom to have a tub of hot water brought into the nursery and all the children well scrubbed in soap-suds. As I was the eldest, my turn came last, and on this particular evening, while Anne and Lucretia were passing under nurse's vigorous hands, I drew my little chair close up to mamma, who was holding the baby. I was so still that she hardly observed me; she scarcely took her eyes from the baby's face, and I noticed that she looked very sad, very pale, very tired. I remembered how she had watched over him day after day and night after night, and now if God should take him away after all! I had not forgotten for a moment what nurse had said in the morning; I longed to ask mamma what *she* thought, but I dared not, for the love and pity that I felt for her. The baby was very quiet; he was very thin, dark circles surrounded his eyes and lips, his face had a touching look of suffering patience, and something strange and stern seemed to flit across this pitiful expression. It was the shadow of death, but I did not know it, only my whole heart was drawn towards him with a love full of awe. There was a harmony of expression between my mother's face and his. They seemed to understand each other, and I felt like an intruder, an outsider. "Mother," said I at last, in a low, timid voice, and biting my lips hard to keep from crying, — "mother, do you think our baby will die?"

My mother cleared her throat, but there were tears in her eyes as she answered in an equally low tone, "I hope he is better to-night."

28

"O mamma," said I, rising and holding out my arms with an irrepressible longing, "do let me take him just for a moment; he's so light, poor little thing! and I do want you to give him to me this once, only this once; I'll be very careful." I had never been allowed to touch him, but without a word mamma answered my request by putting him into my arms.

He was a very light weight, and mamma soon saw that I was quite able to carry him slowly up and down the room. The short twilight of a February night was deepening, but I thought it strange that the darkness should settle *first* on his face.

It was very late before I was put to bed, and I fell immediately into a deep sleep, from which, however, I at last woke with a violent start and with all my senses in full activity. A candle was burning in the room, and this of itself was so surprising a thing to me, who always slept in the dark, that I sat up instantly to investigate the matter. I became conscious that there was a mysterious movement in the house. I heard the rustling of dresses, doors quietly opening and shutting, and my father's voice in a low tone, in conversation with another voice which it was strange to hear in the night. "Why," thought I, "there's Dr. Savage."

Just then nurse came in eagerly but gently, and began to look for something in a drawer.

"Is the baby worse, Mary?" I inquired.

Mary wiped her eyes on her apron, she did not seem astonished at my being awake, but she told me, with her usual air of authority, to "lie still and go to sleep again," and that the doctor said "baby would not live till morning." She then hastened away.

My power of feeling had been exhausted the previous evening, and, strange to say, it was my imagination which was most affected by what Mary had told me; undefined ideas floated before my mind. "What is death?" I thought. "Does the baby know what is happening to him? Is God perhaps waiting for him at the front door, or would he send an angel instead? Perhaps Dr. Savage's horse sees the angel just as Balaam's ass did." I looked down upon little Anne, who slept tranquilly by my side.

"O, Anne, Anne, Anne," thought I, "how little you know —" *What it was* that she did not know I could not have told, I only dimly imagined. I fell back upon the pillow, and the thought came over me that God might be waiting in our very room. I had been taught that He was always about us; now I realized His presence, and shivered at the grandeur of the idea. In the midst of my exaltation I dropped asleep.

When I awoke it was Sunday morning, the room was full of sunshine, and not a breath of air stirred the slender honeysuckle branches which were trained over the window. The few winter birds had finished their morning songs, and it was not yet time for the sound of church-bells. It was wonderfully still without and within. "It is because God has gone, and taken our baby with him," I thought, and a deep solemnity took possession of me. Little Anne was still asleep; she had not stirred since I last looked upon her by candlelight. I glanced round the room, everything was as usual, even to our Sunday clothes placed in order on the chairs. "Ought we to wear our best frocks now our baby is dead?" I thought.

I lay quite still till Mary entered noiselessly. Her face was quite enough. I knew what had happened, though I asked no question, spoke no word, and the business of dressing passed in perfect silence. When the last curl had been rolled over Mary's finger, she said, "Your mamma wants to see you in her room, the baby is dead."

Mary led me to my mother's chamber, and left me at the open door. The heavy mahogany cradle stood in the middle of the room, and in it was laid a beautiful waxen image of our baby. The curtains were down at the windows, the blinds drawn; it seemed as if the darkness which had settled first upon his face the past evening was loath to leave him, and hung about him last. My mother sat on one side of the cradle, my father on the other. He was in deep black, she in pure white. I saw all this at a glance. Mamma held out her hand to me, her face was swollen with weeping, yet there was nothing sad about it, it was full of resignation. I advanced as if weights were attached to my feet, but the moment she touched me, a rush of feeling swept over me, and I wept a flood of tears. Mamma talked to me cheerfully as I leaned against her, and told me that our baby suffered no more, he was happy with God; she tried to make me comprehend the difference between body and soul. I was secretly conscious that she was endeavoring to make the idea of death pleasant to me. She wished me to kiss the cold face and touch the cold hand, that I might lose my dread of a corpse. I knew her object, though I had no dread. I believed all she told me, but still I thought it was a pity that God had set his heart on the baby when there were three girls to choose from. Little Anne was brought in, and Mary put her down by my side; she looked at the baby, and then her eyes slowly turned first upon mother, then upon father, next upon me, and finally back again to the cradle. "We must not make any noise till he wakes up," she whispered, and went out of the room on tiptoe to find her playthings.

For two days my little brother continued to stay

with us, lying in his coffin, which was placed in the best chamber of the house, a very neat and a very white room. The curtains and coverings were white, and a tall white bed stood in a corner with curtains that looked to me like clouds. On the mantel-piece there were two tumblers, full of purple and yellow amaranthus. I remembered how Mrs. Mason, our old landlady, had gone stooping about the garden one windy day of the last autumn, picking them from under the dead leaves, and groaning a little over each one because every *stoop* cost her a twinge of rheumatism. They had blossomed about the time of our baby's birth, but, frail as they looked, they had outlived him.

It was February, but already a few snowdrops and pale crocuses were shivering on their delicate stems in the grass-plot before the house. Mamma made us gather some of them and strew them over the baby's breast, which was as white and cold as the wreaths of snow among which they had bloomed into chilly life. And at last a carriage with white horses took my father and mother and the little coffin away to the churchyard. I saw it drive off with a sharp pang at my heart, but, child as I was, I soon forgot it in looking, with Anne, at the pictures in "Buffon's Natural History," which was opened for us upon the sofa.

The next summer we were to leave England for America. As the time of our departure drew near there was of course a great deal of bustle and excitement; people came and went, orders were given, boxes packed, consultations held. Anne and I played out doors all day long, and everybody who was to stay behind did all that was possible to spoil us, because we were going away. We had no lessons, and our felicity was only interrupted by the necessity of trying on a great many new frocks, during which process I have no doubt we tried the patience of the dressmaker even more than she did ours.

One afternoon, just before we sailed, mamma sent us with Mary to the churchyard, that we might see for the last time the place where our little brother was laid. We were full of spirits, and went skipping and shouting along the lanes till we were quite tired out

35

at last, and quite ready, when we reached the church-yard, to stand silently by Mary's side and look down upon the baby's grave. A large flat stone covered it, and while I was trying to spell out the inscription "Samuel, only son of Samuel and Mehitable G...... Born...... Died......" it suddenly grew very dark, and when I looked up I saw a great black cloud hovering directly over us. I remembered that it had followed us all the way from home, and I thought it was remarkable that it should stop just when we did.

"Mary," said I, "I dare say that cloud is going to America just as we are, and it has come to bid my little brother good by before it flies over the water." Just then a few great drops fell heavily upon the gravestone. "See, Mary," I cried, "it sheds tears for our baby." And I was secretly mortified and ashamed of myself that I could not weep too. I kneeled down upon the marble slab, and by a sort of clairvoyance I seemed to look through it, down, down under the earth to where my little brother was lying, pale, beautiful, and quiet, with the snowdrops still drooping on his breast.

III.

TWO LUMPS OF SUGAR.

I WONDER if all children dislike their nursery as I did mine? The word *nursery* always makes me think of the great big room at the very top of our house at M......, covered with a faded carpet, which, having first adorned the drawing-room and then my mother's chamber, had finally mounted to the third floor, where it enjoyed a threadbare old age, and found itself daily strewn with battered dolls, broken tea-sets, torn books, carts without wheels, and horses without legs. This room was also a sort of hospital for decayed furniture, and there was quite a large army of veteran chairs and tables, whose limbs we children were allowed to amputate at pleasure. No sooner did we enter the house from school than Mary was directed to take us "right up to the nursery, where we could make as much noise as we chose!" As if there could be any pleasure in making a noise on such easy terms! So in the nursery we passed our days, strictly forbidden to go "down stairs" on any pretext. This injunction of mamma's was a very wise one; she did not wish us to play with the servants, about whose characters she knew nothing, and she thought it right to accustom us to some restraint, and not allow the whole house to be disturbed by our noise and restlessness. She provided us with plenty of playthings; we went to school, and walked daily in the "Infirmary Gardens." We had sufficient variety, and I ought to have been contented; but Rasselas grew tired of the Happy Valley, and *I* grew tired of my nursery. "Down stairs" gradually grew into my ideal of Paradise: it was from "down stairs" that Betty the cook used to send me magnificent yellow chariots, cut out of huge carrot, with round slices of the same for wheels; from "down stairs" ascended at five o'clock fragrant odors of dinner and a cheerful sound of laughing and talking whenever the dining-room door was open; from "down stairs" rousing knocks at the front door announced ladies in rustling silks and waving plumes, who came to visit mamma; the hall lamp "down stairs" glowed like a sun, and dazzled my eyes when I peeped over the banisters; even puss ran away from us whenever she could, and scampered "down stairs." I did not blame her; I myself lingered there always as long as possible on my way from a walk or from school. I admired everything there: the mahogany stand in the entry, from whose branches coats and hats seemed to be growing, while canes and umbrellas sprouted from its feet; the oval dinner-table, which the housemaid was often setting towards evening, where the candles shone so brightly upon the snowy cloth; the silver and glass, and the decanters of port and sherry, whose colors were as bright as the purple and crimson jars at the chemist's round the corner. Everybody drank wine in those days. Ask your grandfathers, my little children, if they do not remember how it sparkled by candlelight when they went to dine with their old

friends, and sang songs and told stories and pro-
posed old-fashioned toasts. Yes, even the distant
sound of Betty poking the kitchen fire was pleasant to me as I lingered " down stairs." Above all,
it was the region which mamma inhabited, and
which she adorned by her graceful presence. We
were very proud of our mamma ; she was acknowl-
edged to be the " handsomest mother in school,"
as my schoolfellows used to express it.

Sometimes, when there was company at dinner,
little Anne and I were sent for to come down when
dessert was carried in. On such occasions Mary
would curl our hair in precisely the same number
of curls, pull the bows of our sashes out very wide,
charge us not to turn in our toes, and to be sure
and walk into the room hand in hand. Some gentleman guest generally took us, one on each knee,
trotted us to London and back, gave us raisins, in
spite of mamma's anxious looks, and perhaps in-
cited us to be so boisterous that we were finally
despatched in disgrace up stairs again, and put to
bed " out of hand," as Mary used to say.

I remember *one* wet Sunday evening, when I had been all day in the nursery and was more than usually anxious to go "down stairs," more fretful and cross than was customary, so that Mary exhorted, remonstrated, scolded, finally assuring me that I was the most troublesome child she ever saw, — which I dare say was true. At length, as a last resort, she called me up to her, and whispered that if I would be good, she would show me something beautiful after the children were put to bed. Her mysterious air fired my imagination, and I became "good" at once, and desperately anxious to assist her in undressing the little ones. How impatiently I watched her as she rocked Lucretia to sleep in a low rocking-chair with a drowsy creak, singing through the five long hymns without which "Miss Lucretia never got *sound*." You may be sure I held my breath, and would have stopped the beating of my heart had I been able, during the ticklish process of laying Miss Lucretia's head on the pillow, when she was very apt to wake up again and cry for the repetition of a dozen verses at least! At length,

41

the room being still, the fire renewed, the hearth swept, Mary took the candle and went down stairs, promising still, in a whisper, to show me the beautiful *something* when she should return from her tea.

Left alone in the nursery with the dim red fire-light, I fell into a very grave mood. Fantastic shadows flickered along the walls as if they had taken advantage of Mary's absence to come out and warm themselves. A gentle rain and wind struck the windows lightly, as if some sorrowful, weeping, sighing spirit were quietly trying to undo the fastening, and come in to warm itself also. I stared into the fire, and the whirling smoke carried my childish fancy with it, up, up, I did not know where, but I was completely absorbed in wondering about it, and very happy when Mary came back with the candle and a thick gilt book in her hand. She opened it at a place marked by a rich watered ribbon, and with something quite solemn and ex-pectant in her manner, laid it upon my knee. It was a picture of little Samuel kneeling in his bed with clasped hands and upward look, and Mary

42

read to me in a low voice the verse printed underneath, "Speak, Lord, for thy servant heareth." I
was completely fascinated by this picture, and gazed
fixedly upon it; in the uncertain firelight close to
which I held it the features seemed to change expression and the lips to move. Mary thought me in
a promising mood, and as she was a pious girl she
tried in her simple way to explain the story of Samuel. I understood her literally, and was very much
interested in the fact that God called not only Samuel, but all little children as young as Samuel, if they
paid attention and listened for his voice. If they did,
she emphatically added that they "would be good
forevermore." I pondered long over this, wondering how it happened that I, a very light sleeper,
who waked up instantly if our cat mewed, or a
mouse squeaked ever so slightly, should never have
heard in the night that extraordinary sound, the
voice of God! I was resolving to be more attentive
in future, when a dreadful thought occurred to me.

"Mary," said I, "how old was Samuel when God
called him?"

Mary was putting new shoe-strings into our shoes, to be ready for the walk to school next day: " I disremember," she answered shortly, and then, looking at the picture with a puzzled face, she added, " Four years old, there or thereabouts, I should say, miss, by looking at his curls and his nightgown."

Yes, it was as I feared ; Samuel was only four years old, while I was six, — too old to be called of God ; I had not listened for his voice at the right time, and now it was too late ! I was very indignant with Mary for not telling me all this long ago, and a pang of disappointment shot through me, followed by a reflection which, I am sorry to say, comforted me a little ; as I had not been " called " I was not obliged " to be good forevermore."

I suppose Mary was pleased at seeing me so quietly and thoughtfully pondering over her words, as I sat in my little chair by the nursery fire, for, after she had finished putting in new lacings to our shoes, and set them side by side under the edge of the bureau, with a clean pair of socks laid upon each, she said, " And now, miss, I'll read you some-

thing." She produced from her box a tract with
crumpled leaves, which she smoothed on her knee,
as she told me it was all about a very little girl
named Martha, who was called of God in her cradle,
and who died when she was younger than I. Poor
Mary, she would have been shocked had she known
what was the only clear idea I received from all
her simple talk, that I was too old to begin to be
good, and that it was of no use to try, since I
had not been "called" in proper time. I went to
bed in despair, and with a feeling of great dislike
to the more fortunate Samuel and Martha; luckily
at six years one sleeps off despair and dislike. I
only remember one of the anecdotes which Mary
read to me concerning little Martha of the tract,
on that Sunday evening. She was a very poor
child, to whom a bun was a great treat, but somebody once gave her one, and in a transport of
pious self-denial she ventured into the street and
offered it to the first person she met. This person
chanced to be a lady carrying a small basket in her
hand, out of which she produced two Queen-cakes,

which she gave Martha in exchange for her bun. I resolved that I would some day imitate this act of virtue on Martha's part; it would not be *too* difficult even for one who had not been "called," and I did so after this fashion.

Every summer a great fair was held in M......, and, as we were always living in the country at that season, an old bachelor friend of my father's once begged permission to take me to the city during the fair, and show me all its sights. I was six years old, as my mother reminded me, when she straightened the bows of my sash, and tied on my hat, in preparation for this great event, — too old to disgrace my family by putting my elbows on the table, or kicking the "rungs" of my chair, for I was to dine with good Mr. Swan at his bachelor lodgings in M....... I was in an agony of impatience, for he was waiting for me at the door in his gig, but my mother would not let me go till she had carefully smoothed on every finger of my gloves, pinned one clean handkerchief to my side, as we were not allowed pockets, and concealed another in the bosom of my frock, "in case of nose-bleed," she said, for her previsions were wonderful; at the same time giving me a long list of directions for my behavior, something after this style : —

What to do.	*What not to do.*
Always to say "Please" and "Thank you," at table, and	Not to say "I don't like turnip," if any was put on my plate.
To eat what was put on my plate without remark.	Not to take large mouthfuls.
To keep tight hold of Mr. Swan's hand in the streets.	Not to stand on the outside of my feet.
To wash my face and hands after eating.	Not to let a thief snatch away my handkerchief.
To lay my hat down in a clean place.	Not to ask Mr. Swan to buy me anything at the Fair, but not to forget to thank him if he did.
To pull up my socks when necessary.	

Generally.

Not to be troublesome.

All the events of this day are impressed on my memory, as it was the first I ever spent away from my mother and the children.

What a day it was! On looking back to it, it

47

seems to have been a week long, at least. We made first a tour of the stalls which lined the streets, and poor Mr. Swan must have had a hard time of it in pulling me along, for, O, how fascinating they were! What a delicious smell of varnish from the cheap toys; how I longed to take "between my two motherly arms" all the dolls in pink and blue glazed cambric; how I longed to stop and work the little churns, and set out the little tea-sets, and draw up and down the lambs on wheels! How I trembled with excitement when Mr. Swan showed symptoms of noticing any particular toy, I was so hoping he would buy something for me! I had to bite my lips in order to obey mamma's injunction not to ask him to do so. At last, probably noticing my anxious face, he took up a toy windmill, evidently with the intention of investing a penny therein for my benefit, when lo! the vanes came out in his hand, as he tried to whirl them. This seemed to me such a dreadful accident that I did not wonder at the clamor set up by the woman who kept the stall. "There, take your penny," said Mr. Swan, handing her that coin and the broken windmill together. "These wretched toys are not worth buying, my dear," he said to me; "you don't care for them, do you? they would not hold together till you got home." I could not tell a lie, so I said nothing; but I was terribly disappointed. I thought I might at least have had the broken windmill which he had paid for. The tears came into my eyes; I think he noticed them, because I was obliged to turn my head so awkwardly in reaching for my handkerchief wherewith to wipe them away.

We happened to be just passing the last stall, and Mr. Swan, casting a hurried glance around at the treasures displayed there, hastily produced another penny, and purchased for me a — fly-trap, in the shape of a miniature house painted yellow, with a red roof, a green chimney, and a blue door which slid up and down, and formed one end of the house. I understood the construction of this artful trap in a moment. "See, O, see, Mr. Swan," I cried joyfully, "you pull up the door, and if it don't stay, you can tie it to the chimney, you know — O, I forgot — if you please — No, thank you very much — and then you put a bit of sugar on the floor inside, and when the fly walks in to eat it, you shut down the door as quick as a wink. O, what a useful thing! so much usefuller to have than just a plaything only to play with, — a baby plaything," I added, feeling all the dignity of my six years. "Our flies are getting to bother us, Mary says, and I can catch them in my trap, and help mamma very much. How glad she will be, when she sees me bringing home such a useful thing!"

To insure the safety of this valuable article, Mr. Swan put the fly-trap into his pocket to carry home for me. I was afraid he might accidentally sit upon it and break it, and I wondered if it would be polite in me to remind him of it, if I saw him about to seat himself.

Then this kind friend took me to the Menagerie; it was Wombwell's celebrated Menagerie, which made a yearly progress through the country during the season of fairs, and this was my first visit thereto. Mr. Swan was very tall, and he perched me upon his

shoulder, so that I could gaze into the very eyes of
the elephant, and look down upon the lions and tigers,
while other children were pushing their way to the
ropes in front of the cages, and standing on tiptoe
to catch a glimpse of any tawny paws and noses that
might be thrust between the bars. And what extraordinary pockets Mr. Swan had! If he was tall,
they were long, and as inexhaustible as his good-
nature. He had nuts for the monkeys, apples for the
elephant, bits of sugar for the gazelle, buns for
the bears and for me; moreover, he let me give these
nice things to the animals all myself, and even when
the elephant felt in all his pockets for broken biscuit
in the most coaxing way, he would not give him a
bit, handing up to me every fragment instead; for
which I made a sort of table out of the top of his hat.
I thought this self-denial of Mr. Swan's more wonderful than anything Martha of the tract had ever done.

The two famous lions, Wallace and Nero, were in
this Menagerie. When we stopped in front of their
cages, I bent my ear down towards Mr. Swan's chin,
uplifted sideways, that I might listen to the story he

told me of these lions being once forced by sporting men to fight with bull-dogs. Wallace, who was very savage, killed all *his* dogs easily, but Nero refused to hurt those who attacked him, contenting himself with just keeping them at a distance with long sweeps of his huge paws. My heart warmed to Nero as he lay asleep in his cage, making a pillow of his mane, that looked as amiable as if it had been made of ringlets, while Wallace, next door, was grumbling to himself in short snaps and snarls. In a few moments a keeper entered Nero's cage, and began to tease the poor tired creature by shaking his paws, pulling his ears, and stretching open his eyes and mouth, which made the wondering crowd do the same as they stood looking on. Then the keeper stepped upon the prostrate body, as if it had been a platform, and made a speech which I could n't understand, the words seemed longer and harder than any I had yet come to in my spelling-book. Then he got down again, and threw open the cage door, and after some hesitation a man and woman came up out of the crowd, and, entering the cage, took seats on the lion's body as if it were a sofa. Then I remember that my heart began to beat suddenly and violently, for Mr. Swan asked me if I would like to do the same, and then I was somehow lifted and carried and handed about, and at last felt myself, I hardly know how, sitting on the warm spring-seat of the lion's back, which went up and down, up and down, like clock-work under my light weight. I was alone in the cage, for the keeper had withdrawn for a moment to heighten the effect of the tableau, and the people outside clapped and hurrahed. I recollect venturing to pat the lion with a very small hand, which I suppose he scarcely felt; and, finding him so quiet, I wiped a little place on his warm side with my handkerchief, and stooped to kiss it. There was another burst of cheering and clapping, and then I found myself walking away again on Mr. Swan's shoulder.

He must have had quite enough of me by this time, for I recollect playing quietly in the kitchen through the afternoon, with Mrs. Airy the landlady; she had flying cap-strings and curls, and a breezy way of running back and forth between the range and the dresser, which made her name very appropriate. She was making cake, and as I believe I had never eaten a piece of cake in my life, the very smell of it, as it was baking, was a feast. Mrs. Airy's was an area-kitchen, and a flight of steps led from the doorway up into the street. I amused myself by standing on these steps with my eyes at a level with the sidewalk, and imagining how the world must look to such short-legged creatures as dogs and cats; then, returning to the kitchen, I stood upon a chair, and tried to get Mrs. Airy's point of view by making myself as tall as she was. I was already tired of my fly-trap, for I did not know what to do with the flies after I had caught them, and they hurt my feelings by buzzing inside to be let out. I determined to turn it into a summer-house for our gardens, and keep the door permanently tied to the chimney.

I had never been allowed to stay in the kitchen at home, and I suppose I troubled Mrs. Airy extremely by asking, like Miss Edgeworth's Frank, all sorts of questions about the simplest kitchen-furniture which

I saw there for the first time. At last she gave me a bunch of raisins, and told me to go to the top of the steps and eat them, while I might also be watching for Mr. Swan to appear with his horse and gig to take me home. Hardly had I taken my seat on the top step when I saw a poor woman coming slowly along, and with a covered basket on her arm. Instantly I thought of Martha of the tract; here was my opportunity, I would give this poor woman my bunch of raisins, and probably get in exchange, out of her basket, something I liked much better. No sooner thought than done. As the woman passed me, I jumped up and offered her my raisins, saying, as sweetly as I knew how, " Here is something for you." The woman looked surprised, but she took the raisins, and in a whining voice she drawled out, " May the Saints be your bed, my purty dear," and popped them into her basket, but alas! without offering *me* anything in return. Indeed, there seemed to be nothing in the basket but scraps of dry bread and cold potatoes. I stood indignant, after the woman had walked off, feeling that I had been cheated out of my raisins, and much disposed to cry about it, till it suddenly occurred to me to go down and tell Mrs. Airy what I had done. She would think me so good, as good perhaps as Martha of the tract, and would probably give me some more raisins at least, perhaps something even nicer. So down I went to Mrs. Airy, who was sitting in a rush-bottomed chair, with her floury elbow on the pie-board, deep in the perusal of the Cookery-Book. As she did not seem to notice me, I was obliged to speak first. "What do you think I have done?" I said.

"Not torn your frock, nor lost your handkerchief, I hope," she answered in quick alarm.

"O, no," I said, with a smile of conscious virtue, "no indeed, but — I have given away my raisins to a poor woman."

"Dear me, what made you do that?" said Mrs. Airy, getting up from her chair, and walking away.

"Now she is going to the closet to get me something nice," I thought to myself, and I added aloud, "Yes, all, every one, — every — single — one." Mrs. Airy by this time had reached the kitchen-sink.

"Won't you come and pump for me, there's a good child, and I'll just wash my hands and arms here," she said. I jumped up with alacrity, thinking that she was washing her hands with the intention of rewarding me from her store of goodies. Impatiently I waited while she wiped them on the kitchen roller, and then — she turned about and walked up stairs. In short, I got nothing by the loss of my raisins except perhaps a good night's rest, for probably they would have given me the nightmare if I had eaten them.

To return to the nursery, from which I have wandered a good way. Its windows looked out upon a desolate wilderness of house-tops; the roofs and stacks of chimneys grouped about in confusion reminded me of the appearance of cities after they had been shaken by earthquakes, as I had heard the children at school describe them, out of their geography lessons. Nothing appeared on these roofs but cats and sparrows, watching each other furtively, and sometimes a mason in a paper cap who worked on the chimneys, or the occasional apparition of a man's head popping up from a scuttle, like a Jack in a box. I soon got tired of scanning the house-tops, and found it more interesting to look down into the yards below. A certain poor woman used to come into our yard daily, a wretchedly poor woman, all skin and bone, with a faded rag of a petticoat, barefooted, and with the remnant of a shawl over her tangled hair, and she brought with her always a skeleton baby, with claw-fingers like a little bird's foot; weak and thin as it was, the poor mother could not have carried it, had it been any heavier. The poor woman would stand in the yard, in a diffident, doubtful way, as if ready to vanish at a word, and Betty, the cook, would appear with such "cold victuals" as there were to spare. With the deepest interest I would watch the poor woman's trembling hands, as she rolled the scraps of food in her ragged apron, for basket or bag she had none, courtesying to Betty in humble thank-fulness. Then my beautiful mother, so young and blooming, in her white dress, would be seen walking slowly along from the kitchen, carrying a glass of milk for the poor baby. The wretched little thing would lift its head from its mother's bony shoulder, and stretch out those two claw-like hands, as soon as it saw the milk. And when once it had raised the glass to its pale mouth, nothing could induce it to stop drinking till every drop was drained. It held the cup to its lips with all the strength of starvation. Sometimes my mother let me come down and stand by her side and look at this poor baby, and never shall I forget the heart-rending tones of the poor mother when she made her invariable speech of thanks to my mother : "God bless you, ma'am, and may you never want ! "

I happened to be with my mother on the day when this poor woman came to our home for the last time before we left England. The memory of her grief, her agony, haunts me still. Where she found the flood of tears she shed, in her poor wasted body, I cannot imagine. Wringing her hands, she cried out, over and over again, "O ma'am, you are going away ! Baby, our only friend is going away ! — O, what shall we do, what shall we do ? We shall starve to death, baby, we shall starve to death."

What misery existed among the poor of England in those days!

Our next neighbor, Mr. Anthony, had a very large house and a very large yard, which at certain times of day swarmed with children, for Mr. Anthony had fourteen boys and girls, as near of an age as they could well be. I soon selected my favorite from among them, a little girl rather older than myself, about eight or nine years old, whose movements I watched with great interest; she laughed louder than any of her brothers and sisters, climbed higher, jumped farther, and I often burst into involuntary loud laughs, myself, at some of her gymnastics. She was so handsome, too, I thought; as painters say, her coloring was very fine, for her eyes, her hair, and her silk apron were black, and her lips, cheeks, and merino frock were red. I teased Mary to find out for me what her name was, and she told me it was Hem'ly, which mamma said meant Emily. We sometimes met in the street, when Emily would return a frank greeting to my smile of recognition. In fact, she had not romped all her life with fourteen brothers and sisters without acquiring a great deal of confidence, but this I knew was necessary to a heroine, and the heroine of my childish imagination Emily Anthony forthwith became. At last her mamma sent her to our school; fancy my delight when I found her there one morning, occupying the seat next to mine, and staring about her as composedly as if she were in her father's yard.

The divine Emily tolerated my devotion to her very good-naturedly, and allowed me to wait upon her, to wash her slate, pick up her handkerchief, find the place in her spelling-book, and *prompt* her when we stood up to recite, which I did at the imminent risk of being overheard by the teacher, and condemned to wear a sampler pinned to my waist for the rest of the day as a punishment.

My beloved friend had also a trick of perpetually nibbling sweet things when she could get them, and I was very jealous of the caresses which she bestowed upon those of the girls who gave her sugar-plums and candy. I secretly determined that when I grew up I would open a confectionery store, and that Emily

Anthony should sit behind the counter all day and help herself at pleasure to the stock in trade. But, alas! I was not obliged to wait so long before gratifying her propensities; a great temptation fell in my way.

About this time mamma began to allow us to take tea with her in the parlor, and, after tea, she was accustomed to send me to the sideboard to put away the tea-caddy, sugar-bowl, and other small articles. The very first time mamma put this sugar-bowl into my hands I wished that I could give Emily just one lump, and though I drove away the thought, it grew upon me every day, till, at last, one unhappy evening, in a sudden impulse yet with great trepidation, I seized a bit of sugar from the bowl just before shutting the sideboard door, and concealed it in the bosom of my frock, for mamma did not allow us to wear pockets. My terror was excessive, for I thought mother knew everything, and that she would see the lump of sugar right through my dress, lying against my palpitating heart. I kept in the dark as much as possible, and as soon as I went up stairs I hastened to deposit my ill-gotten treasure

in a little tin teapot belonging to my doll's furniture.

That night I had very bad dreams, and next morning would have given anything to have been able to
return the lump of sugar unobserved, but, as this
was impossible, I did what I thought the next best
thing, and carried it to Emily; whatever remorse I
felt was changed to joy when I beheld the satisfaction
with which she crushed it between her little white
teeth. She rewarded me by making me a present
of an old needle-book with the flannel leaves torn
out, and, better than that, she bestowed caresses upon
me profusely, and begged me to bring her some
sugar next day, averring that it was "a deal nicer
than comfits." My enthusiasm was completely
roused, and I felt it was both an honor and a duty
to steal sugar for Emily Anthony. When papa at
tea-time read from the newspaper an account of a
poor woman who was arrested for stealing a loaf of
bread to keep her child from starving, and who
defended her conduct boldly before the magistrate, I
found a strong resemblance between her devotion to

her child and mine to Emily. It was some time before I was convinced that mamma was not ubiquitous, and that she was entirely unsuspicious of me, but as soon as I discovered that I was mistaken in the extent of her discernment, I rushed to the other extreme, and began to entertain a profound contempt for it. I helped myself to sugar before her very eyes, and after depositing it in my teapot, would dance about her like a wild Indian, rattling it in her ears, and begging her, urging her, to guess what was inside.

But, one night, having grown very bold, I helped myself at the table to *two* lumps of sugar, each larger than common ; mamma's back was towards me, and I thought myself quite safe, but before I could pop them as usual into the bosom of my frock, she turned suddenly round and bade me make haste, and carry away the sugar-bowl. Forced to obey her, I closed a hand awkwardly over each lump, and took up the bowl between my two fists.

" Peasy," said mamma, " that is a very careless way of taking things up, you will certainly drop the sugar-bowl; put it down and then open your hands, and carry it in a proper manner."

This, alas! I could not do without betraying myself, and mamma, seeing my embarrassment, opened my hands for me, and saw my guilt at once.

I cannot describe the violent and agonizing change in my feelings. I had never dreamed of tasting a morsel of the sugar myself, and so great was the ascendency which Emily Anthony had obtained over my imagination, that I thought it impossible to do wrong in serving her, and I had gloried in my sin, entirely unconscious that it *was* a sin. But now my conscience woke up strong and suddenly from its lethargy, and lashed me with a whip of scorpions. The scales fell from my eyes, and I saw myself a thief of the basest kind, who had deceived mamma's unbounded confidence, and had forever lost all right to her esteem and affection. In the midst of my misery papa entered the room.

" See," said my mother to him, " see this little thief. I trust her with our property, and this is the way she rewards us."

She exhibited my passive hands, with the half-melted sugar still adhering to the burning palms; if I could have summoned an earthquake to destroy the city of M......, and bury me under its ruins, I would gladly have done so.

Papa ordered me up stairs at once, and indeed I did not feel fit to stay in their presence, and hardly dared to enter the once despised nursery, which I now felt was far too good a place for me. I kept aloof from little Anne, who was eating bread and milk in her low chair, with puss watching at her side. I would not even have polluted the cat by stroking her.

For two days I was in disgrace, and confined to the nursery. Papa and mamma never spoke to me, nor caressed me, but looked at me with grave and anxious faces. Mary followed their example, and I thought puss walked past me with a contemptuous wave of the tail. Little Anne alone treated me as usual, and seemed quite unconscious of my position; but I suddenly found myself grown very much older, and while I respected her superior goodness, I looked down upon her as upon a very little child. When any one entered the nursery, I rushed to the window and looked out perseveringly till the person was gone, but you may be sure I turned away my eyes from Mr. Anthony's yard. I could not endure the thought of Emily and her fourteen brothers and sisters; I wished myself a sparrow or even a rat, anything but a wicked little thief. Mamma made me learn a number of hymns and verses applicable to my case, which I repeated to her in an agony of shame, feeling that they were written expressly for me, and wondering how the authors could have known so long ago that such a naughty girl would be born into the world. I was not allowed to say my prayers at mamma's knee, nor did she kiss me when I went to bed, where I cried myself to sleep as softly as possible, with my head under the bed-clothes; it was a comfort to put Anne's hand under my cheek after she was asleep, and to soak through her little night-gown sleeve with my tears. As for the tin teapot, I hated the sight of it; I bent and pummelled it into a shapeless mass, and threw it among the cinders under the grate. My first gleam of pleasure was in seeing Mary carry it away unconsciously to the ash-bin.

On the third morning papa entered at an unusual hour, and, calling me to him, took me on his knee, and talked to me gravely but very kindly about my sin; he told me that if I was heartily sorry for it, God would forgive me, and that *they* would receive me back into favor. Never had repentance been more sincere than mine, and he was convinced of it. The tears which his sympathy caused to pour over my cheeks washed away all the unprofitable bitterness of my grief, and left me with an earnest desire to do better and repair my fault. When mamma came in she kissed me, and spoke to me as usual, and I felt as happy as Christian when his bundle fell from his back. Mary immediately became very gracious, and puss amiably accepted a bit of my breakfast which I ventured to offer her.

I had a great many unhappy doubts as to whether mamma would find it possible to have full confidence in me again, but though my feelings were *grown up,* my language was the language of a child, and I had no power of expressing them to her. I remember nothing more about Emily Anthony, except that I returned her the dilapidated needle-book. She had entirely lost her influence over me, and in future I could watch her gambols in the yard with a stern and sarcastic composure.

IV.

WELLINGTON.

ALL children love animals; the baby six months old plunges its hands rapturously into poor kitty's fur, and endeavors to get her head into its mouth, while the little brother next in age drags her away by the tail and tries to make her comfortable by rocking her violently in the cradle, knocking her poor head from side to side till she springs out with a loud "miau" and takes refuge under the sofa, from whence no tears and entreaties can coax her, no trailing strings, no rolling balls, no poking of broom-handles, can dislodge her, and the poor babies are heart-broken. *My* first loves were the rats in our yard at M....... Safe in my nurse's arms I used to watch them dodging behind the boxes and barrels; now a long tail, now a sharp nose and bright eyes, would pop out, as they squealed and tumbled over each other. In vain I held out my piece of bread to them and called out in my most fascinating tones, " Here, yat, yat, yat," I could never teach them to come and eat out of my hand. We had to put the bread down, and withdraw to a respectful distance, if we wanted to get a full view of my favorites, who were pretty sure, after a careful inspection of the premises, to rush out and drag it away in a little whirlwind of dust, without so much as a look of gratitude. I could not blame their bad manners, for Bob, our big mouser, would generally be sunning himself on the shed, or on the stone sill of the kitchen window, and the rats and I were equally afraid of him. He was an immense yellow cat, who could stretch and swell himself out as big almost as a lion, I used to think, and his buff-ringed tail would wave and quiver till I felt as sure it would bite me as if it had been a poisonous snake. I did not like to be left in the room alone with him, for he claimed the hearth-rug as his private property, and if I ventured to approach it, he greeted me with a growl like distant thunder; he had besides

71

a way of fixing his eye upon me in a very unpleasant manner. I was so afraid he would mistake me for a rat, though I tried to look as little like one as possible.

Mamma had a canary who sang delightfully, but he was hung so high up in a lofty room, to be out of Bob's reach, that we never got much acquainted with him. I thought he was a great deal nearer to heaven than he was to us, and that he was God's bird, singing his beautiful songs for God alone. He used to flutter and chirp in a terrified way when mamma took his cage down to clean it, till at last the morning came when he was found lying very still on the bottom of it, with his slender claws held up piteously, very like a certain picture in our "Death and Burial of Poor Cock Robin." Anne and I endeavored to bury him according to the forms prescribed in that book. While she "carried the link," a lead-pencil with a bit of red rag tied to one end, I was "the owl so brave, who dug" Canary's "grave," in the scrap of flower border in the yard. Afterwards, wrapping him in a doll's muslin apron for a pall, and shutting

73

him up in a paper box for a coffin, I carried him to
the grave in my mouth, and waved my arms in imitation of the wings of the kite who bore Cock Robin's
coffin through the air in a similar manner. We set
up a piece of broken slate for headstone, on which
we got mamma to write the following couplet: —

"Under this stone
Lies our canary's bone."

You see he was so small we thought he could not
have more than one bone in his body. The first rain
washed away the epitaph, but before that time we had
forgotten all about him.

At our country lodgings we had Moll to play
with. She was a white mastiff of great strength and
size, who bore our teasing as patiently as she bore the
awkward gambols of her puppies. We endeavored
to assist her in their education by trying to teach
them to stand on their legs. With infinite pains we
set them up on their feet, stretched very far apart, and
when they reeled and tottered and rolled over, we
patiently began again. We thought they improved

73

under our instruction every day, and took great
credit to ourselves when at last they could stagger
along without tumbling down the whole distance
between Anne's lap and mine, fully a quarter of a
yard. But, alas! just at this period of advancement
the puppies were removed and given away, and Moll
howled in concert with us.

Moll died one winter while we were in town, and
next spring we found Fan, the spaniel, reigning in her
stead. But we did not like her; she was always
scampering about with her nose to the ground, tongue
lolling out of her mouth, and her long chocolate-
colored ears flapping against the side of her head like
winglets. She used to burst in upon us like a little
hurricane, upsetting our sedate dolls' school just as
our pupils were studying their lessons off bits of
newspaper pinned to their knees, or scattering our
dinner dishes nicely set out upon a cricket, just as we
— Mrs. Howard and Mrs. Fitz-Clarence, as we called
ourselves — were sitting down to an elegant repast.
Out of sheer disgust to Fan, we began to take a great
interest in a poor forlorn turkey, the only turkey

among the poultry which pecked about the barnyard
industriously. It looked very patriarchal with its
bald head and long red beard, but its behavior was
very undignified, it was so timid and bewildered. It
was always standing on one leg in an anxious manner, and squeezing under the hedge, or huddling its
feathers in a heap as it clung to the lowest branch of
an apple-tree. It hovered behind the other fowls
when we went out to feed them with crumbs, and if
we threw a handful far enough to reach it, it ran off
in a fright, and the big rooster would walk up in a
stately way and swallow every morsel, the poor turkey
looking dismally on from behind the pump. We
pitied it because it had no mate to gobble at and to
strut before, and we paid it great attention, so that at
last it came to eat fearlessly out of our hands, and
kept us company whenever we played out of doors,
walking after us with its light springing step like a
friendly spy. Fan used to rush upon it sometimes,
when the poor thing would look just ready to faint
away ; but we in turn charged upon Fan with pinafores outspread and armed with sticks, and happy

was she who managed to box Fan's ears. We comforted our poor turkey with bits of bun, and it bowed its head gratefully before us, picking them one at a time from our laps. From being "the thinnest turkey in the four kingdoms," as Mrs. Mason averred, it became the fattest, its feathers grew sleek and shining, it stood firmly on two strong legs, instead of on a single trembling one. Mrs. Mason called it *my* turkey, that is, she said I should have it for my birthday present. My birthday occurred late in the autumn, and we were to return to M...... soon afterwards. Anne and I laid a hundred plans for conveying our turkey to the city per basket or meal-bag, and for constructing him a coop in the yard, well barricaded against the rats; we hoped he would not be much afraid of them, he was already beginning to make a faint show of standing his ground against Fan, which promised well, and, in good hopes that his courage would grow as his body had done, we agreed to call him Great-Heart.

On the afternoon before my birthday we went out to see Great-Heart, and to give him some cold boiled rice as an earnest of what we would do for him when he was really our own bird. While he was eating we smoothed his feathers and told him wonderful stories about M...... and the yard, and the coop that was to be, carefully avoiding the subject of rats. It was very cold, and our teeth chattered as fast as our tongues, but Great-Heart was now too plump and sleek to mind the cold, so we assisted him to mount his favorite perch in the barnyard, and ran in to pick out our very prettiest bit of ribbon wherewith to decorate him next day.

On the following day, therefore, we woke up as bright as the morning sun without and the sparkling fires within; we put on new frocks, and mamma gave us our best playthings, while the lesson books were laid away on an upper shelf. As soon as we had swallowed our breakfast, we ran into the kitchen, ribbon in hand. There was to be company at dinner, so Mrs. Mason and her maid Jane were very busy making puddings and tarts and cakes, but they left off to smile upon us, and to wish me many happy birthdays; kind Mrs. Mason wiped the flour off her hands,

77

and brought from the depths of her pocket a crockery sheep with deep red spots on his sides, lying under a green crockery tree, which she told me was a birthday present, while Jane gave me a peppermint heart of the largest size, which she took from between the leaves of the cookery-book. I kissed them both, mistress and maid, standing on the points of my toes.

"And you said I should have Great-Heart, the turkey I mean, on my birthday, did n't you, Mrs. Mason?" said I, "and he's mine now, ain't he? so I'm going to see him."

"Yes, deary, I said you should have him, and I've kept my word, sure enough; he's just out doors there if you want to look at him."

Off we ran again, calling "Great-Heart! Great-Heart!" as fast as we could, for it was not an easy name to speak fast, and at last running up against him before we noticed him. What a terrible sight met our horrified eyes! Poor Great-Heart tied up against the wall by both legs, a great slit in his neck, which hung down limp and lifeless, and a small

78

puddle of blood underneath. He was stone dead. Anne burst into tears of grief, and I into a storm of passion. I flew back to Mrs. Mason, and seized her fiercely by the dress, quite speechless with rage and horror for a moment.

"O deary, the flour! the flour! don't touch me, it will be all over your frock, and what will mamma say?" cried she, holding her hands up out of my reach.

"I don't want to touch you, you bad woman!" I broke forth, suddenly letting go my hold of her. "How dared you kill my turkey, you cruel, wicked woman! I hate you with all my heart, and I'll break your sheep's neck just as you broke poor Great-Heart's." And thereupon I flung the crockery sheep across the kitchen, where it was broken into a dozen pieces against the bars of the grate.

"Deary me!" said poor Mrs. Mason, astonished, "why, didn't you know I always meant to give you the turkey for your birthday dinner? Didn't I say so, deary? Why, I thought you'd like it, so I did. Now don't ye cry, don't ye, dearies, and I'll give you old Top-Knot herself instead. She 's a deal nicer old creetur than that stupid — "

" Hold your tongue !" cried I, fiercely. " What," thought I, " cut Great-Heart's throat and then insult him ? " My grief redoubled, but my fury was soon over; and I wept as piteously as Anne did. I began to be a *very little* sorry, too, that I had broken my present, but I would not allow it to myself.

The company arrived, excellent friends of ours as well as of papa and mamma. I received some pretty books and games, and my sorrow was somewhat soothed, especially as mamma sympathized with us very much, when she found how we had been deceiving ourselves. If she had known of my bad behavior to Mrs. Mason, she would have sent me immediately to ask pardon, and that I vowed I never would do, never, never; but I was not put to the test.

At dinner-time we sat one on each side of mamma, and a great way from the turkey, which was placed before papa. We did not turn our eyes in that direction, but, in spite of this precaution, a good many tears dropped from them, which we wiped stealthily away on our printed pocket-handkerchiefs. Papa had the good sense not to offer us any of his dish, and we managed to get half-way through dinner decently. We listened with a great deal of indignation, and some pride also, to the careless comments of the company upon the superior size and flavor of poor Great-Heart. "What did they fatten him upon, I wonder?" said one of the guests.

"Buns," said papa, seriously.

This was too much. Anne and I looked at each other, and ran out of the room to cry again, sitting on the top stairs with our heads despairingly against the banisters. Here Jane found us when she came to bring us each a little fan made from the poor turkey's feathers, and here Mrs. Mason found us when she came to tell us how sorry she was for us, and to hope we would not be vexed with her any more. I suppose we forgave her, for I remember we spent the evening in her room, both of us in her lap, while she rocked us in her rush-bottomed chair, and sang to us "Lord Lovel," "The Soldier's Return," and other ditties. After all, if a great shadow darkened this birthday, there were patches of sunshine too.

Papa always had a fine horse. Not always the same, for he often changed his favorites; and though we used to cry heartily when the old pony was sold, we welcomed the new one with delight, and he soon trotted and cantered as far into our affections as his predecessor. It was a fearful joy to pat him with loud hard pats, and to cry courageously, "Poor fellow, good old fellow, stand still, old boy!" while at the same time we kept one eye upon his ears, and if he pricked them up ever so little we were quite ready to start back with a cowardly scream. When we were riding, we gave most of our attention to the horse; it was so curious to watch him, shut up between the shafts, whisking his tail over the reins, nodding and wagging his head, as if he were talking to himself, and turning first one ear and then the other stealthily round if we spoke but a single word; such pretty ears, too, so nicely lined with soft hair

like a couple of bird's-nests! Of course we always
spoke of him while riding in the most complimentary
terms, and what moments of suspense we endured
after papa touched him with the whip, lest he should
take it ill and tumble us all out. It was curious
also to see the great spreading veins under his thin,
shining skin, branching all over him like a vine, and
how this glossy skin would quiver convulsively if a
fly did but touch it with one tiny foot.

"Flower" and "Spring" were the first of papa's
horses which I remember; they were both white,
and they glimmer like four-footed ghosts among
the dim and broken recollections of very early childhood. And then, distinct in outline and color, comes
Wellington, bright bay Wellington, the Bronze horse,
the Enchanted horse of my young days. He was an
old blood horse, an old trooper, and had belonged
once to a cavalry officer who had ridden him into
battle. He must have been an animal of uncommon
character, for he seized upon my imagination like a
human being, and indeed I sympathized with him
far more than with most human beings who fell in my

way. I thought I had never seen any *man* so gentle, elegant, and high-bred as Wellington; and his face had a pensive sadness of expression which I fancied was owing to his having looked down so often upon wounded and dying soldiers. When he stood immovable in the paddock with downcast head, I believed he was recalling the memory of some fierce charge, and that he saw bleeding men among the daisies and buttercups. I *almost* saw them there myself.

John Cookson, the groom, bestowed a great deal more care upon Wellington than Mary, his sweetheart, vouchsafed to *us*. It took twice as long to comb *his* mane as it did to curl our two heads, and the scrubbings *we* endured were nothing to what *he* had to bear. Our breakfasts were much easier to prepare than his warm mashes, and there was a great deal more fuss made about the set of his harness than about the set of our frocks. If he refused his supper, papa and Mr. Mason and John and half a dozen loungers, with their hands in their pockets, went into the stable anxiously to look at him and prescribe for him; if we could n't eat ours, mamma only said, "O, the children are tired, put them to bed and they 'll be hungry enough in the morning." Putting us to bed was the sovereign cure for all our troubles bodily and mental, and we found, on inquiry among our school-fellows, that other children were similarly afflicted. It was well enough in winter, but to go to bed at six or seven o'clock of a mid-summer evening, when the furniture in the chamber almost floated in a strong sea of sunshine, this was really abominable, and it made us highly indignant. " What, go to bed in the broad day? the woman's cracked!" said the little cobbler in the play to his wife, who was recommending him to lie down. We were too polite to express such an opinion about mamma, whatever our private feelings might have been.

Putting us to bed, however, was *one* thing, and going to sleep was another; this was often impossible, though we tried our very best: in vain we balanced ourselves on opposite edges of the bed, as far apart as possible, lest we should disturb each other, repeating in monotonous tones the stupidest of our poems, our last spelling lesson, or counting over and over up to the very last number that we knew; in vain we shut our eyes so tight that they ached, and tried to think of nothing at all, some cunning ray of sunlight would be sure to make itself small enough to enter by slipping its seven colors one at a time under our eyelashes, and dazzling us so with rainbow effects that we were obliged to lift up our eyelids to let them out again.

Then all sorts of wide-awake sounds came to us through the open window: Brindle coming up from pasture, and lowing all the way, so that we could tell, by the increasing loudness of her "moo-hoos," just when she got to the big gate, to the cart-path, to the bars, and so on fairly into the barnyard; the hens clucking about the kitchen door, where Jane sat singing "Black-eyed Susan"; Mr. and Mrs. Mason discussing the prices of butter and beef in the porch, from whence ascended a fragrant odor of tobacco; papa's approaching gig-wheels grinding the gravel in the avenue, the sudden pull-up, the loud "whoa," the stamping of John's big boots as he came out to take the horse, and then a smell of tea and muffins creeping under the door, and through it all Mary in the nursery, and the swallows under the eaves "hush-a-byeing" their little ones, who seemed to be as far from sleep as we were. We could not bear it any longer.

"Anne," I would say, "I think we ought to sit up as long as the sun does; let's play."

Play we did. The chintz counterpane, with its knots and bunches of flowers, made a delightful garden of Eden when spread on the floor, and covered with the animals out of our Noah's ark. The white bears, and those of the creatures whose names we did not know, we banished to the arctic regions, represented by our two pillows, which made admirable snow-banks. We, Adam and Eve, sat under a tent of sheets, and surveyed our domains with pride, but soon, like Adam and Eve, longing for more experience, we ventured to pop our little nightcapped heads carefully out of the window. We drank in great draughts of summer air scented with clover;

we heard the cuckoo's faint voice from a distant
grove, and the far-off chimes of the church; we
saw the long soft cloud-drifts which the sun would
by and by turn into crimson and golden pillows for
his sinking head; and then we watched the black
and red caterpillars which crawled along the win-
dow-sill and up into the tall honeysuckle. Everything was serious and beautiful to our young eyes.

Once in a fit of recklessness Anne dropped an
elephant on father's head, he happening to stand in
a very tempting position just below us. We were
in a great fright lest we should be detected, but
for all that we could not forbear keeping our heads
out of the window to watch the effect. Luckily the
little big beast rolled gently from the crown of papa's
hat to the brim, and then slipped down his back
into the middle of a rosebush.

"Those swallows are so troublesome," said papa,
looking up to some nests under the eaves, and
walking quietly away, at once to our great relief and
sorrow !

We had to make a great many awkward attempts

before we could rearrange the bedclothes after our nightly plays, but we slept soundly at last in spite of the wrinkles. One night, just as I was dropping into a dream, I heard Mrs. Mason's voice calling to John.

"John, there's eggs wanted for breakfast, and the master says you may take Wellington the first thing in the morning and go round to the water-mill farm. Perhaps you'll get some there, there's none hereabouts, and mind you start by sunrise. I'll leave the basket on the kitchen table. You know the road, don't you? down Sweetbrier Lane, and past the great willow by the brook — and —"

I remember no more, only that the great willow waved its arms through my dreams, the brook rustled, the mill-wheel turned; and when a stupid half-awake early fly buzzed against my face at four o'clock the next morning, I started up, half expecting to hear Mrs. Mason finish her directions, and then becoming conscious that it was just about the time when John would be getting ready to fulfil them. Hark! yes, that was John walking across

the kitchen in his stocking feet; then I heard him
whistling merrily in the yard, and pretty soon the
whistling was accompanied by sundry snortings and
stampings, and a great knocking against the stable
door, by which I knew that both Wellington and the
currycomb were taking part in the trio, though John
was obliged to interrupt it very often with loud excla-
mations of "Mind yourself now! Hold up your head!
Stand still, you—" John and Wellington were pre-
paring to go down Sweetbrier Lane, and so on to the
water-mill farm. These words suggested a hundred
confused beautiful pastoral images, and, let come what
would, I determined to be of the party; and this was a
desperate resolution for a little girl brought up in the
extreme of English regularity, reserve, and seclusion.
In the first place I had never dressed myself in my
life, but, nevertheless, I scrambled into my clothes as
well as I could, buttoning them in front and then
turning the buttons round to their proper place behind, before attempting to put my arms through the
shoulder-straps, which of course went snap, snap, one
at a time, each snap costing me the most dismal

forebodings. What *would* mamma and Mary say? When it came to frock and pinafore I had to rouse Anne. I can see her now, kneeling on the edge of the bed, her uncurled hair drooping over the little collar of her nightgown, sleep and wonder contending in her eyes, while with her small fingers she patiently made a succession of hard knots in each string for want of ability to *tie bows*. Equipped after a fashion, I seized my hat, and ran softly out of the light room into the entry, where the darkness still seemed to be dozing away in the corners, and where I could hear from the open chamber-doors the long breathing of sleepers which seemed to hush the very walls and furniture into repose. I had never noticed before that the stairs creaked at all, but now, as I went down, stumbling over my shoe-strings, each step brought out a creak as loud, I thought, as a pistol-shot, and I wondered how the darkness could doze, and the people and the house sleep on through it all. But they did.

All the dusky way from my bedroom to the back door my heart beat with fear, and I suspected that I was a very naughty girl, but as soon as I stepped out, for the first time in my life, into the early glory of a summer's day, my whole being blended with it, and I felt " good " because the morning was so good, and I was a part of it. I had played " Garden of Eden " so often, that the idea of Eve came at once into my mind, and I confusedly half realized what were her sensations when she walked out before breakfast on her first waking in Paradise; "only," I thought with a sigh, " she had no buttons, or strings, or shoulder-straps."

What a singing there was ! It seemed as if every lark, blackbird, robin, thrush, which had been hatched into the world since the creation, was trying to outdo all the rest, each warbling his loudest, right at the broad face of the sun, who, having just cleared the horizon, was stretching forth long arms of light in a morning blessing over the earth. My imagination opened wide and suddenly, like the convolvulus cups in the porch, which, born after the dew, reflected the blue of heaven without its tears.

John's strong white teeth showed themselves in a

broad grin as soon as he saw me, and as he was a thoughtless, good-natured fellow, he made no objection to taking me with him; he knelt down patiently to tie the ribbons of my hat under my chin, not without leaving the marks of his broad fingers and still broader thumbs. So behold me mounted before him on the saddle, holding the empty egg-basket fast in both hands, and my heart fluttering with joy against his arm. Think of being so near Wellington's wonderful ears that I could whisper into them as Tom Thumb did! so near to that cavern of a mouth from whence issued snorts and neighs and champing of bits! But the strength and vigor of the horse magnetized me, as people say nowadays, and gave me courage, so that I felt as brave as the fierce officer who in former days had pricked Wellington into battle with great bloody spurs, and I rode past the duck-pond and the cucumber hot-beds in high feather.

What a view I had from my lofty seat! I no longer envied Tippoo Sultan his white elephant of forty hands high. Could n't I see the whole world stretched out beyond the top of the hedge, as far as Farmer

Greatorex meadows? The number of cottages visible at once was quite beyond my knowledge of counting, and each was decorated with a plume of smoke which waved gallantly in the breeze. Instead of smoke, ivy wreaths were swinging from the low broad tower of the church, like the curls of a green wig on its gray forehead, I thought, and I could see the thick black yew-trees in the churchyard, which refused to smile in the sunshine or to let it warm the cold gravestones over which they brooded. In the horizon the place of the huge manufacturing city of M...... was marked by the heavy lurid cloud that hung over it, covering a world of misery, which I was too young to understand. For the poor in English manufacturing towns starved to death often in those days, and the poor in M...... were unusually numerous and wretched.

But without troubling our heads much about the city of M...... and the misery hidden under that curtain of smoke, John and Wellington and I jogged along on that most beautiful of all the summer mornings that ever shone for me, and drew near the " Flying

Dragon," a wayside public house with a battered sign-
board representing a creature like a winged crocodile,
clawing the air, and breathing out flames; but these
flames, once I suppose of a terrible brightness, were
now reduced to a number of dull red spots, so that the
flying dragon appeared to be suffering from nosebleed,
and the sheep which he carried in one paw looked
very much like a dirty white pocket-handkerchief
wherewith to wipe away the drops. The upper part
of the house was fast asleep, the curtains being drawn
down over the windows like so many eyelids, but the
bar-room was wide awake, sashes thrown up, and the
red hangings, fluttering outward and upward, had been
caught and suspended on the laurel bushes, so that
there was a fine view to be had inside of Betty the
scullery-maid clattering about in her pattens, scrubbing and sanding the dirty floor, while the shining
bottles and glasses on the shelves looked down upon
her with clean complacency. The tall clock in the
corner ticked at her in tones of exhortation, as if it
said, " Bet-ty, Bet-ty, work, work, work, work." It
stood on four legs like four ninepins, and seemed to

be holding up its scanty skirts out of the way of the
mop. John had pulled up so near the window that
Wellington could put his head in, and smell daintily
at the geraniums which stood upon the broad ledge,
and which he was too well bred to bite, while I studied
the wonderful clock, with the day of the month just
coming into view under the minute-hand. Over its
face was a small painted heaven, Gothic-shaped,
through which rolled a painted moon, waxing and wan-
ing after the example of the real moon, and, being then
only in its second quarter, it looked at me roguishly
with one eye, hiding the other behind a painted
thunder-cloud, a few inches square. This clock played
a tune always before striking, and I devoutly hoped
that John would prolong his chat with Betty till that
time; indeed, there seemed every prospect of it, she
was leaning so comfortably on her folded arms between
the pots of geranium, whose scarlet flowers were no
redder than her cheeks. But suddenly distant doors
were heard to open and shut, and a shrill voice to cry
" Betty! Betty!" " The missus!" said Betty, and
ran off in one direction, while John spurred his horse

in the other, and so violently that the basket came
very near flying out of my hands and up among the
branches of the old oak which shaded the porch, with
its benches and settles, and whose arms always seemed
to be akimbo, they were so **crooked.**

On we went in the shadow of the young plantations
which bounded the domain of D...... Park, listening
to the cawing of the **rooks, above the** loftiest trees
in the **park.** Suddenly **we** heard the distant voice of
a lark pulsating in mid-heaven. **Since** then I have
heard **the** enchanting carillons which **float** over the
land **from** steeple **to** steeple in Belgium, so ravish-
ing that one might believe the angels **who** descended
to sing of "Peace and Good-will" had taken up their
abode **in** these watch-towers of the Lord, and that
while **the bells** ring out time to men's ears, *they* sing
of eternity to men's souls. Yes, I have heard them,
these chimes of bells and spirits, and I thought of the
lark that I heard singing in D...... Park, between me
and the sky, on that morning of **my** childhood. It
reminded **me of the time when** *my* soul was lighter
on its wings than then, and mounted up higher to meet

the descending sounds, which seemed to me to slide from heaven.

I never thought to ask John which was Sweetbrier Lane, for the road was all so beautiful that it deserved to be called so from one end to the other. Gentle verdant slopes stretched away to the right hand and to the left, and where they met each other, foot to foot, a little thread of a brook gurgled; so tiny it was that the sun would have dried it up in a minute, had not the water-plants obligingly held their broad leaves over it like so many green parasols. The cows stood up to their knees in clover, so did the apple-orchards. At one place we passed the smallest of cottages hidden under the biggest of cherry-trees, where two little white-headed boys were tying up deep red cherries in bunches, for sale. They had a long new board, full of holes, into each of which they stuck a bunch of cherries; it was quite like a new kind of garden, perhaps like the ruby path in Aladdin's garden of jewels, I thought. The boys had on queer-looking velveteen trousers, doubtless made out of a pair of their father's. We saw him getting over the stile, pipe in mouth, a great burly man; one pair of his breeches would have clothed all Tom Thumb's brothers and sisters. "Weel done, little chaps," said he with gruff good-humor, as he passed the busy white-heads; they looked up with pleasant smiles in their light blue eyes.

All the pretty social flowers and low-running vines, which in England love to stand by the roadside and see the world under the shelter of the hedge, had their twinkling eyes wide open this morning, as if there were no such creatures as sturdy laborers with hob-nailed shoes to punish them for their curiosity. John held long conversations with some of these early workmen, often in the Lancashire dialect, of which neither Wellington nor I understood a single word. So much the better, since I could imagine, if I chose, that they were saying eloquent and poetical things to each other, in harmony with the glory of the morning and of my happiness.

At last we came to Nanny Baggerly's cottage, which stood on a bank near the highway. Nanny Baggerly was an old woman who took, for a small

price, poor sickly children to board, from the M......
poorhouse. They were brought to her sallow, ema-
ciated, sunken-eyed, afflicted with rickets, with sores,
with ophthalmia; fatherless, motherless, utterly help-
less, utterly patient. She did what she could for
them; the food she gave was of the plainest description, but it was wholesome; she turned them out into
the fresh air, and spoke to them roughly, but kindly
and cheerfully. Many a little one recovered; and
from lying languidly all day in the sunshine following with sad quiet eyes the gambols of the others,
and shrinking up against the wall if big Tommy or
rude Sally came within a rod of him, began at first
to creep a little, from daisy to daisy perhaps, as he
gathered and held them loosely in his nerveless fingers; then from creeping to standing, though big
Tommy might have blown him over with his breath
even when so far advanced as that, and at last, grown
strong and stout, you might have seen him racing
about with the rest, and returning rude Sally's fisti-
cuffs with interest.

Many were so fortunate as to die and be buried in

a pauper's grave, but it was a pauper's grave in the country, and dear mother earth knows no distinctions. She takes the poor little pine box and the coarse shroud which wrap the shrunken beggar child as tenderly to her bosom as the mahogany coffin and the flannel garments of the rich man's heir. The violets and buttercups on one grave soon nod merrily to sister violets and buttercups on the other, and the bees and butterflies hover over both. The big ash stretches a long arm over each, and the birds don't care on which branch they happen to sit and sing. The autumn wind wanders and moans around each little mound, and strews it with dead leaves, and in winter one snowy winding-sheet folds them both. Perhaps the little beggar and the little heir walk together, hand in hand, in the spirit world.

It is good for that child to die who lies unwept in its coffin, and from whose meek head no hand cares to sever one lock of hair.

Death seemed very far from Nanny Baggerly's cottage, however, on the morning when John and I rode past on Wellington. Nobody was visible but a strong brown boy eight years old, who was hacking away sturdily at a big cabbage in the little garden.

"They'll be having that cabbage for dinner," quoth John. "Peter, I say," raising his voice, — "Peter, have you got the taste of that porridge out of your mouth yet?"

Peter turned fiercely round and brandished his knife, but he could not resist John's good-natured grin; he broke into a sheepish laugh, and ran into the house as nimbly as a squirrel.

"What do you think the likes of them gets for their breakfasses, miss?" said John, looking down at me. "'Milk!' says you, I'll be bound! Very little of that they see; some of 'em don't know the taste of their mother's milk even, poor lambs! But old Nanny stirs 'em up a mess of oatmeal porridge in the pot, she do make it thick and stiff, and them young uns hovers round the chimney corner, watching her stir and stir, and sniffing up the steam till she has to tap their heads with the porridge stick, and drive 'em out on to the step where they and the chickens huddles up and peeps in together. You

see the chickens has the inside of the pot to themselves after it's done with, and Nanny sets it out
doors. When the gruel is so thick that the porridge stick stands up straight in it, Nanny says to
herself, 'That'll do,' and she pours it out over a
big pewter platter, bigger than Mrs. Mason's chopping tea-tray."

"Bigger than *what?*" said I in great wonder,
and then bursting out laughing. "O John, it is n't
chopping tea-tray, but *Japan* tea-tray."

"Well then, *jobbing* tea-tray, it's all the same,
miss, and then she holds out quite a fagot of
spoons, and says, 'One at a time, boys.' They
march in, take their spoons and range themselves
in a circle round the platter, which stands on
the floor, and then that good old creetur wipes her
hands and her snuffy old nose on her apron, and
says grace like any parson; the 'grace before
meat,' you know, miss, in the prayer-book, which
begins — which — which, in short," says John, "I
disremember; but it's a good rule, miss, of old
Nanny's, this saying of grace, it's pious, and it

gives the porridge time to cool. She gives her 'A — men' loud and solemn, like the clerk, and then she cries quite cheerful, 'Fall on, boys, and see which of you 'll eat the fastest!' and faith, that would be hard to say; it 's *gape* and *swallow* with 'em all, and rattle your spoon against the platter, till one would think drum-major and all his boys was coming down the road. Nanny don't set their dish out to the chickens, you may be sure; the boys cleans and polishes it better than soap and sand.

" Well, now, that little chap Peter is the smartest and cleverest of all Nanny Baggerly's young uns. It 's he that makes the fire, and picks up chips, and brings water, and digs taters and cabbages, as you see, miss. And when good charitable ladies call and bring penny tracts, wot 's his name's hymns [Watts], and papers of buns, and all the rest of the children huddles into a corner with their fists in their mouths and their eyes fit to drop out of their heads with staring, it 's Peter who comes for'ard, makes his manners, and says, 'Thank you, ma'am; I 'm

sure you're very good, ma'am.' Even Mr. Whitelock the clergyman don't dash him; he takes to the
gold spectacles and the gold-headed cane quite natural. He says off the Creed and Ten Command-
ments better than you do, miss," said John, laughing,
' begging your pardon, I'm sure, miss, for saying so.
He can tell Mr. Whitelock, 'Who was the first
man?' 'Who was the first murderer?' 'Who was
Noah?' 'How old was Methusaleh?' And he
can tell his own age and his name too, and that's a
wonderful piece of knowledge for a workhouse boy.

" Well, t' other morning, just as the porridge was
smoking in the platter, and old Nanny had got as
far as ' A—men,' a gentleman on horseback stopped
at the little gate. He looked up and down and all
round as if he'd lost his road, and then, turning his
head towards the cottage, he called out, ' Hallo there,
good people!' It was plain to see that he wanted
to ask his way to some place.

"' Run *you*, Peter,' said Nanny; ' it 's only you
can make a decent bow and give a decent answer to a
stranger.'

" Peter looked first at the porridge and then at the gentleman. He was one of those petickler old bachelor gentlemen who wear drab gaiters and starched neckcloths and pinks in their button-holes; who carry their elbows turned out stiff, their whips straight up and down, and their heels sticking against the sides of the horse. Just one of the gentlemen to ask forty questions about nothing at all, — Who lives here? Who lives there? Where does that road take you? Where does that lane go? How many miles to M...... and B...... and W...... and Lord knows what number of places besides.

" 'Oh, oh!' thought Peter, 'the porridge will all be eaten up long before I get through answering *that* old cove.'

" Besides being the smartest boy of the lot, Peter was always the hungriest, and that morning he was mighty sharp set, for he'd been working in the tater patch and had just run in, his feet covered with black mould. 'Halloo!' cried the gentleman again, in a terribly loud voice and quite purple in the face with impatience. 'Halloo up there! are ye all deaf or dead?'

"'Goodness gracious,' cries Nanny. 'Run this blessed minute, Peter, or he'll ride up to the door over the cabbages.' Peter casts another glance at the porridge upon which the boys were just throwing themselves, and then without saying a word he claps his bare foot right down in the middle of the dish quick as a flash, and then runs off like a greyhound.* There was the print of his foot left in the porridge just as black and distinct, thanks to the garden mould, as them pencil picters of Mr. Freeman's; heel and toes and the marks in the rough skin, all as natural and as dirty as life. More than that, Peter had cut his foot against a sharp stone so that it was bleeding a little. That looked as if one had used a red lead-pencil as well as a black one about that queer drawing. If it had not been for the *red lead-pencil*, I do believe the boys would have devoured every morsel of Peter's foot, but they could not stand that. So they ate round it as close as they could get, and polished the rest of the dish as usual. When Peter came back he found his foot waiting for him, right in the middle of the shining

* A fact.

platter; he swallowed it all down in a moment, a toe at each mouthful; there's no such word as dirt for hungry people, miss. Old Nanny chuckled, and laughed to herself over the boy's coolness; she took him one side, and gave him a hunk of barley bread to top off with. Old cove gave him a penny too — Hulloo, what's *that?*"

We were on the M...... turnpike, just where the road makes a sudden bend, when we heard a great confused noise which made John stop short in his story. I immediately thought of the drum-major whom Nanny Baggerly's children imitated so well, but on turning the corner, behold! not only the drum-major and his boys, but the rest of the band, and half the boys and girls of M...... besides, who were following a regiment just marching out of M...... on its way to distant quarters. It had been a very popular regiment with the townspeople, and though orders were given for an early march in order to avoid leave-takings, a crowd of the sorrowful populace came out for the sake of accompanying them a few miles on their way. It was an interesting sight. Many platoons and here and there a whole company marched along with stern resolution, doing their best to keep up the dignity of the procession, looking neither to the right hand nor to the left, and carrying themselves, as well as their guns and accoutrements, with military uprightness. But great numbers of the younger men had left the ranks, and were walking arm in arm with groups of workmen and artisans. Many reeled and staggered very unsteadily, and there was a great deal of embracing and shedding of tears, as much owing to gin as to sentiment. Some soldiers were beset by clamorous and eager men, low tavern-keepers and the like, seeking to get their bills paid, — dirty strips of paper which they flourished before the eyes of their debtors, who walked doggedly along, secure of tiring out these creditors at last. Often you might see a young girl weeping, with her apron thrown over her head, her lover doing his best to comfort her, and thrusting the last penny of his pay into her passive hand. One poor thing, who stood quite near us, sobbed out so pitifully, over and over again, " I 'll never see you any more, Jem ; you 'll never come

anigh me again, Jem; you'll soon forget me, Jem;
will you be sartain sure to write me Jem?" that I began
to cry too, and to shout out a series of answers to these
sorrowful forebodings by way of consoling her. " You
will, he *will,* he *won't,* he *will.*" There was such a
noise that nobody heard me but John, who laughed
heartily. Now and then we passed a couple taking
leave of each other in a more sensible way, married
people evidently, with little ones fast asleep at that
time probably in some garret at M....... *She* perhaps
was to keep a shop or take in washing while her hus-
band was off sogering, and they were too busily talking over their plans to have time or heart for grieving.
Their anxious faces would have been less sad to look
upon if they had overflowed with tears.

Looming up high above all heads towered the great
baggage-wagons, packed, piled, and heaped with lug-
gage, which was strapped, chained, and fastened in
every conceivable way. All sorts of pots, pans, and ket-
tles dangled and jangled from the sides with stunning
discord, while perched upon the very top sat the few
soldiers' wives who were allowed to follow the camp,

rolled up in scarlet cloaks with hoods, which were drawn over their heads. Bronzed, weather-beaten women they were, bantering the crowd below with harsh, cracked voices. Some had children in their laps, all were smoking short pipes, and in the violence of their gesticulations they seemed just ready to throw both children and pipes among the joking rabble. Pedlers and venders of all kinds of eatables and drinkables trudged wearily by the side of the wagons, and some half-starved dogs kept equal step with them underneath. You could hardly hear above the din the drums, fifes, and trumpets of the band playing lively tunes to cheer up the spirits of the men. Nobody listened to them except the mob of boys and girls who followed in a sort of long trot, with ragged pinafores and mouths full of toffy.

No common horse could have faced for a moment this disorderly multitude. When quiet people, jogging along in their carriages or on horseback, beheld from afar off a marching regiment approach, they vanished hurriedly down by-lanes and cross-roads, or fairly turned about and rode back as fast as possible.

But Wellington, the old charger, was in his element. The moment he heard the drum and fife he pricked up his ears, and gave a loud snort of satisfaction, which came from his inmost heart, arched his neck proudly, and began to thread his way steadily among the throng. His eyes shone as brightly as the bayonets, as he stared about wistfully among the soldiers, and with short, cheerful neighs seemed to ask, "What cheer, comrades, what cheer?" He looked at the scarlet cloaks and the lean dogs as one who knows them of old, and he showed a noble patience with the teasing rabble, who recklessly tickled him with straws or shook their greasy hats in his face. If a child fell down between his feet, he waited for it to get up; if a man ran against him, he moved carefully out of his way.

In the midst of all this, I hardly know how, we started off full gallop down a shady lane which opened suddenly to the right. When we slackened our pace, the din and dust and tumult had passed away like a dream, and we were crossing the willow-shaded brook according to Mrs. Mason's directions.

The unexpected change made it seem more beautiful even than I had fancied ; the grand old willow hung with a sort of silent passion over the water, as if enchanted with its never-ending story ; some of the boughs trailed out on the current at full length, others only reached down far enough to touch the foaming crest of each little wavelet as it hurried off. The pools were full of fallen leaves, tiny archipelagoes of small green islands, and a few slender bare wand-like limbs moved mysteriously along the water as if writing secrets on its fickle heart. What a curious willow it was ! All the lower limbs brooded in constant shade over the water, and knew nothing but the brook, while the topmost branches, quite out of its sight, grew straight up into the sunshine, and knew nothing but the summer wind which piped merrily to them as they danced.

As we approached our journey's end the hedges began to be full of blackberry-bushes. What child of my age could see blackberry-bushes without think-ing of the babes in the wood ? And as it was my habit to be constantly imagining myself somebody else, of course I immediately became little Jane riding "upon Cock horse" to London before the good robber.

"John," I broke out abruptly, after a few moments of intense thinking, "let's play my brother William is riding behind us, that's the reason we can't see him; let's play the wicked robber is making horrible faces at us over William's head. Let's play that you two ruffians are going to fight, as soon as we get to the wood. How we babes shall cry and cry!" continued I, opening my handkerchief, printed with Dr. Franklin's maxims. "But you must n't mind that, you must go off to get us some bread, and we shall wait and wait —"

During this speech, delivered with great energy, John's countenance had exhibited the extreme of bewilderment, but here a sudden light broke in upon him. "Certainly, miss, with all the pleasure in life. I'll get you a piece of bread the moment we reach the farm, and there's the house, sure enough, before us. Wait? yes, so you *have* waited and waited as patient as a lamb, miss, and very hungry you must be!

How stupid of me never to fetch you a bit of bread before we started! But Dame Jenkins shall cut you off a corner of the brown loaf in a jiffy."

A few rods down a steep winding cart-road, and we stopped at the farmhouse, a low broad stone cottage deep sunk in the rich grass of a little glade which opened out upon the brook. There was just room for the diamond-paned windows to peep out between the overhanging thatch and the profusion of gillyflowers, balsams, and London pride, which blossomed luxuriantly up to the very sills. The walls seemed to have been built for no other purpose than to train vines upon, they were so overrun with homely English creepers, woodbines, honeysuckles, morning-glories, scarlet runners, all climbing in a rich tangle together up over the roof, blossoming among the mosses of the thatch, and garlanding the massive chimney. They hung so thickly down from the porch that Dame Jenkins's white cap was lost among them, as she stood there to welcome us, and only her friendly eyes were visible under the clustering leaves. Two or three blackbirds and finches sung rapturously in wicker cages hidden beneath this greenery; a half-open casement discovered glimpses of a dark oaken-panelled kitchen, every panel reflecting a ruddy gleam of the firelight from the stone hearth. Thickets of laurels, lilacs, rose-bushes surrounded the house, and a pair of gigantic lime-trees hung their branches like a great green dome, high above all, under which the sunshine and fresh air played freely. This was my first visit to the mill-farm, but by no means the last, and I learned its beauties by heart.

John would not let me go into the house with him; perhaps he was afraid I might repeat to his sweetheart Mary the fine speeches he made to Dame Jenkins's granddaughter. He set me on the top of a lofty gate-post under an acacia-tree which swung a heavy cluster of snow-white flowers right above my head; a great yellow bee was thrusting himself into them, and his buzzing made me look up. "O John," cried I, in ecstasy, "isn't it like papa's ruffled shirt-front with a big gold broach stuck in!"

"Eat your bread and butter, miss," said John, sententiously, putting a piece in my hand, which he left me to dispose of at my leisure. It was a piece almost too large for me to grasp, nevertheless I went bravely to work to make it smaller, feasting my eyes all the time upon the charming objects around me, above all, the old water-mill. It stood just opposite to me on the other side of the brook, and at first I was bitterly disappointed to find it was a ruin; the longer I looked at it, however, the more it grew upon me, and at length I became absorbed in it, and understood its picturesque beauty. Its gray crumbling walls were buried in the deep shadow of a very steep bank which overhung the stream, running in at this place like a tiny bay upon a tiny beach of pebbles. The broad sloping roof leaned against this bank, and so much earth had slipped down upon it, that it was covered as thickly with wood plants and wild flowers as the hillside above it, and seemed almost a part of it. Moss dropped from the old wheel instead of water, and blossomed delicately among the crevices of the broken steps. Roof, walls, and wheel, bank and bay and beach, rose before me in the dark transparent freshness of the early morning shadows; the ruin fairly dripped with dew from its hanging masses of greenery. The babbling, brawling brook scampered past it, flouting its patient decay like the naughty boys in story-books — not in real life I am sure — who mock at old age. So I looked, and I ate; and I heard the doves cooing, and the bees humming in the bean-field. Dame Jenkins's granddaughter brought me a glass of new milk; "just from the cow, miss," she said. I was ashamed to say I did not like it, because I remembered that in my story-books, when the children had been particularly good, their mammas would say, "My dears, you have behaved so well that I will let you go down to see Betty milk, and you may take your mugs and get a draught *warm from the cow.*" Drinking new milk was always associated in my mind with excellent spelling-lessons, neatly hemmed handkerchiefs, proper behavior in general. You see my head was full of my story-books, and I could not help thinking of them on all occasions.

When John and I were ready to start again, Dame

Jenkins came out and reached up to us our basket, quite full of eggs, lying among tufts of fresh grass. She talked to me in a very cajoling, flattering manner, and I did n't know whether I ought to feel offended or pleased.

" You 're a dear," she drawled out, in the same sort of voice that Mary used to the baby, " you 're a little angel, bless your bonny mouth and your rosy cheeks ; you 're mamma's beautiful darling, I 'm sure ; did n't you know you was a duck of a pretty little dear ? "

" Yes, ma'am," said I, with modest assurance, feeling some misgivings, though, on account of my hasty toilet.

She laughed, and patted my hand with her skinny palm ; it felt like the claws of the dead fowls which Mrs. Mason sometimes gave me to play with, and which I worked up and down by pulling the tendon of the leg.

John found the basket and the bridle together quite too much for him to manage, and, having full confidence in Wellington, he transferred the latter to me. Imagine my pride and exaltation! I remember nothing of the ride home except a great feeling of responsibility, which made me keep my eyes fixed upon the bridle and the horse's ears; of course I pulled and twitched, and made use of all the jocky sounds and phrases with which my memory supplied me, all of which Wellington bore with the utmost patience. I had enjoyed such a great variety of new experiences, that I felt as if I had been gone from home a great while, and expected to be received with acclamations of delight as a traveller. I had forgotten quite that I was a naughty girl. It was odd to see, as we rode back into the yard, the usual morning's work going on, and to find the day just begun at our house, which had already been so long for me. Jane was sweeping the hall, Anne was coming down stairs in all the dignity of six elaborate curls and a clean starched pinafore. I could see mamma making tea in the parlor. Mary came out, exclaiming, " Well, miss, a fine trick you 've been playing! I wonder you 're not ashamed of yourself, John Cookson! Good gracious, what a dowdy and a fright you do look, miss!"

Mamma scanned me from head to foot, and her glances expressed very emphatically the same opinion. She told me if I ever did so again, she would punish me very severely.

Ah, forgive me, dear mamma, that I felt neither guilty nor repentant. As I stood silent before you, I dare say you thought me sorry and ashamed. The severest punishment, even your serious displeasure, would not have weighed for a moment against the glory and the happiness which I had been enjoying in getting acquainted with nature, and which I enjoy in recollection to this day. I could not help it, mamma! Little children, can you conceive of a little girl so naughty?

V.

BIRKENHEAD.

WE had just taken possession of our seaside lodgings at Birkenhead. Anne and I stood at the parlor window, looking out eagerly upon the river Mersey, that rolled its muddy waters between us and the city of Liverpool. It was alive with vessels of every sort and size, and our active imaginations soon began to personify them.

"Anne," I said, "do you see those very big ships, with their sails beginning to sprout out of their masts? Well, mamma told me just now they are going perhaps to America, where our relations live. Do you see those steamboats, vomiting black smoke, like Apollyon?"

"O, don't!" cried little Anne, covering her eyes, for it so happened that we possessed a very old copy of the "Pilgrim's Progress," with such a hideous picture of Apollyon spitting out fire and smoke that Anne could never bear to look at it.

"Well, then, they're *not* vomiting black smoke, like old Apollyon, but they're nasty things for all that. Mamma says it's rude to point, and every one of 'em looks as if it was pointing out a big, long, dirty black finger at something behind it. O, I'll tell you what. The steamers run about like caterpillars, and the ships are like moths opening their white wings."

"I like the *little* ships the best," said Anne, "let's count 'em. Three over there, and two there, and one just here, and one, two, three, four, — there and there — "

"But see, Anne, two such tiny, tiny black boats, quite close to our side of the river. They're starting to run over to Liverpool, I verily believe; yes, there they go, each of 'em with a great red sail; don't they look like two butterflies sailing on chips? Now I wonder which will get t' other side of the river first? Let's play one of 'em was yours, and t' other mine. One of them has a long red streamer top o' the mast; that shall be mine. No, Anne, you may have it, because it 's the prettiest, and we 'll call him Red Cap, and mine shall be Bald Head, because it has n't any streamer, only that big round knob stuck up on the mast. Bald Head's a Bible name, too; it 's what those impolite children called Elisha, you know, just because he had n't a wig on! Now, Anne, say, — which do you bet will sail fastest, you or me, — I mean your Red Cap or my Bald Head? I 'll bet you 'most any thing Bald Head will get over to Liverpool first. Now what will you give me if he does? Say quick, because I verily believe he 's ahead already."

"O dear," said little Anne. "I have n't a single thing here to give you for a bet. Mamma would n't like me to cut off one of my six curls, or pull out one of my shoe-strings."

"No, child," I cried impatiently, "I don't want anything splendid; just give me that bit of red yarn you 've been twisting up in your fingers, 't will make my dolly a pair of garters. Ah ha! I 'm first,

I'm first! I see old Bald Head's skull bobbing up and down ever so far ahead of Red Cap. Hurra! What do you say now, Miss Nancy? how do you feel now?"

"Why, I *want* you to beat," said little Anne, sweetly. "It is only fair, because you gave me the prettiest boat."

"You darling thing!" I exclaimed. "Now I wouldn't get ahead of you for the world. Here, take back the garters! I don't want 'em. I don't want to beat truly, and I hardly believe I'm going to after all. I don't know what's come to old Bald Head; he's standing still, I verily do believe, and Red Cap's jumping along from one wave to another like a kangaroo. You're going to beat me after all, and I'm just as glad as if mamma had let me eat that dear little raw onion that Mary was going to put into the salad yesterday. Don't I like 'em, — raw onions, teenty taunty ones, I mean! Halloo! why, Bald Head's taken in his sail. Don't his skull look funny atop of that great spine-bone of a mast? He looks like a *skull*enton sure enough, now there's nothing of him but one bare pole. Ain't I funny, Nancy my dear? And you're ahead of me, and you need not deny it, for I'm older than you, and I can see better, for my eyes are larger. Three cheers for Nancy Red Cap!"

Then I snatched off my pinafore, waving it wildly and shouting, exhilarated by the sea-air which blew freshly into the window.

Mary, coming up behind me, seized hold of my pinafore and held it over my mouth tightly.

"What a racket you've been making, you naughty child! *will* you be quiet with your Red Caps and Bald Heads? You're as noisy, I'm sure, as one of them boys that the bear eat up, and serve 'em right, and you too, if you don't behave prettier. You make more noise than six bears growling. I wonder what my last missus would say to you,—my missus before I came here; *your* mamma's too good to you. My last missus, Mrs. 'ixon's Miss Malviny 'ixon, was as quiet as a little mouse. If she ever laughed loud even, her mamma would say, 'Malviny, is that behaving like a lady?'"

I always wondered at the rapidity with which Mary ran off that difficult sentence, which was always at the end of her tongue, — "My last missus, Mrs. 'ixon's Miss Malviny" — for that young lady was so often held up to us as an example that her very name got to be exasperating.

As soon as I could free my mouth from the pinafore and find my breath, therefore, I cried out, —

"Why don't you go back to your Miss Malviny, if you like her so well? I'm sure *we* would n't care, would we, Anne? We would n't cry, we would n't tease you to come back. She's still as a mouse, is she, your Miss Malviny? I should like to be a cat and jump upon her, she'd make a noise once in her life, then; how she'd squeal when I pounced upon her with my claws spread out, *so!*" I added, opening and shutting my fingers, making them look as much like Apollyon's crooked talons, in the picture, as possible, and drawing my face into a likeness of an enraged cat, as I hoped. "And her mamma would peep out from behind the wainscot, — she'll be a mouse too, of course, — and she'd say, ' Malviny, stand still and be eaten up like a lady, and squeak softly.' Then I'd craunch her bones," I added, gnashing my teeth savagely.

Indeed I was a very rude, naughty child, and my impertinence to Mary was very "wulgar," as Mrs. Hixon might have said. But when Mary placed a sudden check on my excited spirits, they were apt to explode in a burst of indignation or vent themselves in extravagant nonsense. This time I rattled on, quite indifferent to Mary's solemn looks of horror: "O Anne, don't you remember at Monsieur Champfort's, how funny it was to see Malvina Hixon dance? How she jumped up, and flung her arms and legs about in such a limp way, like a Merry Andrew! If I had her here, I'd pin her up to the wall, and tie the skipping-rope to her, and jerk her. And her hair, her red hair, Anne, don't you remember how it used to fly, fly up in the air when she was dancing, like a haystack in flames, and how it nearly caught upon the chandelier? O, she'll hang up there like Absalom some day, and Monsieur Champfort will take his fiddle-bow and pierce her."

In the midst of this nonsense I skipped about in imitation of Malvina Hixon, tossing my own hair till Mary's nice handiwork of curls was all in confusion, and getting behind the tables and chairs when she tried to catch me, some of which I overturned in my hurry.

"I don't know what ever will become of you, miss," she said at last, quite exhausted with the chase, —"I don't know, really."

"'You don't know, and I don't care,'" cried I, quoting from "Mother Goose."

"'Don't care' came to the gallows, miss," said Mary, gravely.

The door opened. "Breakfast!" cried I, emerging from under the sofa, where I had taken final refuge. This was our first breakfast at Birkenhead, so of course we had a great many observations to make on the new and strange surroundings. First, we took a prolonged survey of the servant who brought in the tray; she was a hard-worked-looking girl, with a very hurried manner, as lodging-house servants are apt to have. Her cap was crumpled, and her faded dress neatly mended with bright new pieces. As she arranged the table, she glanced at the disordered room, and then at me, with hair and dress equally disordered; she picked up the chairs which I had thrown down in trying to escape from Mary, and then, in a very significant way, she took from the mantelpiece a couple of china shepherdesses, a gilt mug, and a match-box; put them into her blue apron, and disappeared, with another look at my tumbled condition.

"She thinks you look like a regular furniture-smasher, miss," said Mary, "and no wonder. She would n't trust you even with an empty blacking-bottle. She 'll tell her missus of you, and them overset chairs will be put down in the bill. I dare say you 've cracked some of 'em."

This was a mortifying idea, and in order to get rid of it, I began an inspection of the crockery. A little blue landscape was painted in the bottom of each bowl, — blue clouds, blue lake dotted with blue sails, blue mountains, a blue gentleman with a blue feather and a blue guitar, serenading a blue lady, who looked out of the window of a blue tower, shaded by a grove of blue trees. "O Anne," cried I, "this is Lake Como! See, it's printed in blue letters! Don't speak to me; I'm going there."

So I put my face close to the bowl, shading my eyes with my hands, that I might see nothing but the picture. Gradually the landscape enlarged till every feature took the size of nature; the blue melted into greens and browns, and in fancy I was standing on the shore of the sleeping lake, whose wavelets crept to my feet with the softest rippling sound; the mountain flung its grim shadow across the water, while its bare head glowed in the sun; the branches of the Italian pines stirred mysteriously to the hurrying breeze, which set all the light foliage that fringed the bank into a tremor; the lateen-sails bent, some one way, some another; the guitar tinkled; and the plumed cavalier sang out, "O pescator del onda, fi da lin lin la!" I repeated over and over to myself in a whisper, Como! Como! The word contained a thousand pictures for me. Just at this moment Mary inserted the nose of the milk-pitcher between my face and the bowl, and a stream of milk poured down upon Como, drowning the lady and gentleman, overwhelming the tower and the pines, and covering the top of the mountain. It was a second Deluge, and I set myself busily to work with my spoon to eat down to the landscape again.

"I like this house," said I to Anne. "I've looked into the wash-basins, and they're quite as pretty as mamma's wash-basins at home."

In those days it was the fashion to cover the bottom of wash-basins with pictures of beautiful scenery, — castles, parks, rocks, waterfalls, meadows, with sheep and shepherds, forests with deer and huntsmen, — and sometimes with battles, shipwrecks, and sieges, while just inside the brim heavy garlands of flowers, nearly as large as life, were painted, overhanging cascades and fortresses, and, bending down towards wounded soldiers, flying deer or piping shepherds, as the case might be. I had read of the sultan who met with the most wonderful adventures and saw the most glorious sights merely in consequence of plunging his head into a pail of water. For a minute I could very well believe it, for a wash-basin was quite enough for *my* imagination; many and many an hour it spent, tangled up among the flowers, or living and wandering among scenes of indescribable beauty and splendor, all suggested by the pictured bowl over which my dirty face was bending, quite forgetful that it was sent there to be washed.

After breakfast, Anne and I went up stairs to unpack our dolls; papa had lately brought them to us from London, and we were very fond of them; we kept them carefully out of the baby's reach, lest the paint should get sucked off their faces, and we tried to remember not to touch their pink and blue kid arms, unless our hands were clean. We called them Angelina Augusta and Augusta Angelina. In those days names were beautiful in proportion to the number of syllables; now it is different, and all the dolls of my acquaintance are called Sallie and Bessie and Jennie, — names which we should have thought very commonplace.

Angelina Augusta and Augusta Angelina stared very hard with their great unwinking black eyes, as

133

we carried them from room to room, pointing out to them all the charms of our new abode, and holding them up to the window, that they might admire the Mersey crowded with shipping and the heavy red brick warehouses of distant Liverpool visible between masts and pennons.

" How beautiful our dolls do look in their best frocks ! " said I to Anne, " how glad I am they are made of wood, so that they will never die ! I 'm tired of playthings that die like our lame robin and the kitten with weak eyes. Dearest darling Angelina Augusta will keep her red cheeks forever," I added, kissing her passionately but carefully, " unless — O Anne, do you recollect poor Eloisa Matilda, who lay in a pail of water all night, and in the morning had not a bit of face left ? It was just as if her soul had fled."

" I shall teach Augusta Angelina that water is very unwholesome for dolls," said Anne; " we must not tell them when we go to bathe," she whispered.

A slight noise at the door made us look in that direction, and to our surprise we saw a little girl standing on the threshold, her head thrown back, one small foot advanced as if, in the act of entering, she had been transfixed with admiration at the sight of our dolls; we were equally struck with her remarkable appearance, so that we all three remained motionless, staring at one another. Poor Eloisa Matilda herself, after her night in the pail of water, was not more entirely destitute of color than was this child; her lips and cheeks were perfectly white, a mass of thick black hair hung about her, and a pair of very large, very dark, very extraordinary eyes gave a wonderful melancholy to her face, they were so full of a strangeness, a sadness, a horror, almost, of expression. She was dressed in deep mourning even to her stockings, which gave her thin limbs the appearance of bird's legs.

"*I* have got a doll too," said the child, with a sweet smile, which gave a natural look to her old, careworn little face, and restored my courage at once.

"Have you? what is its name?"

"Grandmother," said the child.

"Grandmother! how funny!" said I, laughing.

"Now I call *my* doll Angelina Augusta; what do you think of *that ?*"

"O, I think it's a *beautiful* name," replied the child, with flattering emphasis.

"Well, there are a great many more just as beautiful; I'll pick out one for your doll, if you like. What do you say to Georgiana Cecilia, Seraphina Delia, Annette Amelia ?"

Anne and I, with a view to naming our dolls, had read over the "List of Proper Names" at the end of the dictionary so often, that we could rattle them off our tongues faster even than we could say "Peter Piper picked a peck of pickled peppers." The little girl's wits seemed quite buried for a moment under such an avalanche of long words; then, recovering herself, she answered timidly, —

"My doll is too small to have so large a name, and, besides, I loved my grandmother very much, and when she died and was buried in heaven, — she went up there in a great box, — I called my doll after her, because I love it next best. My doll has a frock made out of one of grandmother's, and she wears a silk handkerchief of grandmother's for a shawl."

"Bring her here, and let me look at her," said I, decidedly. The doll was brought, and proved to be a rag-baby of unusual ugliness, the legs, arms, and top of the head sewed up with the coarsest thread, and a face in the earliest style of rag-baby art, two small dots for eyes, two large ones for cheeks, a perpendicular line for the nose, and a horizontal line for the mouth. But the child hugged it up to her thin neck with so much love and reverence that it grew quite respectable in our estimation, and we lost all desire to laugh at it.

"See," said the child, "how beautifully mother has painted it! The hair is done with ink, — mother dipped the back of the head into an ink-bottle, — the lips and cheeks are of cherry-juice, — mother said she wished she could paint *mine* such a color, — and the eyes are done with indigo out of the bluing-bag."

These were secrets worth knowing. We instantly resolved to begin painting in the same style and on a large scale.

"Who *is* your mother?" I asked.

"She keeps this house," said the child.

"And what is your name?" said I. We had quite forgotten that she might have one as well as her doll.

"Alice Phinney, and I am four years old, — people always ask next, 'How old are you?'"

"Alice Phinney," said I, my mind suddenly recurring to the events of the morning, "you may tell your mother that I am *not* a furniture-smasher, whatever Mary may say, and you can ask your maid to bring back the things she took from the mantelpiece, for I haven't the least idea of breaking them. Just go down and tell them that, please."

Alice opened her eyes, but went down stairs, nevertheless, stopping on each stair to talk to her doll. In a few moments Mary bustled in with a great roll of towels under her arm, and a clean blue-checked apron on. "Come, come, children," said she; "the tide is up, it's time to go down to the bathing-house. Get your hats, quick."

"The tide is up," I repeated to myself, as I laid Angelina Augusta on the bed, and spread a pinafore over her slumbers. "The tide is up." I thought of the five great oceans as displayed on the map, running furiously into half the bays, and climbing half the headlands and cliffs of the whole earth; and all this grand preparation was necessary that two little girls might go and bathe!

I walked along very silently under the influence of this magnificent idea; we went out to the end of a long pier, and entered a gloomy barn-like building. At first, on coming in from the strong sunshine, we seemed to be in total darkness, but how different from the dry brooding darkness of the land! *This* darkness was heavy with damp, and the breath of the sea crept through it; one's blood curdled and one's imagination thrilled at the same time. Most of the light came in with the water under the bathing-house, and soon our eyes were strong enough to discern the short waves leaping up and down against the piles and posts, licking them with their shining tongues, and in the intervals of the quick leaps, little streams of water ran down from the vivid green sea-weed and bunches of barnacles which crowned these posts, making a pleasant murmur in the place, and a sound of silver rippling. We could not form any idea of the depth below us; the shining amber surface of the heaving tide soon melted into brown, and the brown into infinite blackness. The stairs, which led down under the water, grew indistinct immediately, and in a moment vanished from sight; the last visible stair might have been a white rock, a fragment of ice, a mastodon bone, a drowned child even. It looked like anything one chose to fancy. I remember standing in shivering heroism on these stairs, held firmly by Mary, and waiting for the next swell of the tide to overwhelm me. I saw it coming afar off, rising against the narrow strip of sky which gleamed between the building and the water; its sphered crest was lifted to the very foundation of the bathing-house; it grew suddenly dark; I shut my eyes, and the wave went over me. I felt two cold arms of spray, a great wet kiss which covered my whole face, and an indescribable jargon of rushing waters in my ears, like a thousand adventures told in a breath. It was worth to me a whole library of romances.

"Ma'am," said Mary to mamma, when we got home, "Miss Peasy has been as good as gold. She did n't say one word, good, bad, or indifferent, from the time she left the house till she got back. And she took to the water like a — a — young shark or porpoise, ma'am. I never see Miss Malviny herself do better."

We occupied the whole first and second floor of Mrs. Phinney's small house, for mamma liked plenty of room when she took lodgings, but Anne and I could not be satisfied without a thorough exploration of the third story, left silent and deserted while the family who slept there were below. This we accomplished in a series of scamperings up stairs and a good deal of walking on tiptoe after we got there, for we were half afraid mamma might not approve our curiosity. Under cover of doing errands for mamma, we soon got acquainted with the ground-floor, knew the number of pantries, the size of the kitchen, what the cook looked like, and how many eggs she put into our bread-puddings. Mrs. Phinney's own room we never dared to enter, but, as the door was always half open, we could not help peeping in sometimes, if it *was* impolite. It seemed to us that Mrs. Phinney spent most of her time in putting up her hair, which was long and coarse, and continually fell down like a mane over her gaunt shoulders, positively refusing to be kept in place by the broken horn comb with only three teeth left, which the poor woman patiently stuck and restuck into the twisted mass of tresses. There was nothing attractive about this room but its cleanliness; the grate and the brass fender shone with the highest polish, the faded chair-covers were scrupulously washed and starched, the dimity bed-curtains so neatly mended that the patches became quite ornamental. Six varnished shells adorned the mantelpiece from which Mrs. Phinney daily wiped the dust with a small paint-brush. A large feather fan hung on one side of the fireplace, a gilt hearth-brush ornamented the other. Over it a simpering pink-and-white portrait of the departed Mr. Phinney was suspended in a cheap frame, into which a few sprigs of green were stuck. Under this portrait a small clock ticked very loudly, as if it were afraid of the gentleman above, and dared not stop while he was watching it so closely. This room contained what little Alice thought the most beautiful thing in the world, a silhouette of her grandmother in a high-backed chair, with a Roman nose and a tall mob-cap, and the sloping shoulders peculiar to silhouettes.

When I said there was nothing attractive about the room but its cleanliness, I forgot little Alice, who spent most of her day there, sitting in the middle of the floor, with her doll and her kitten. This kitten was called Snowball, and was always described by her as a "white kitten with a blue ribbon round its neck." It did not *quite* do justice to this description, since it passed its nights in the coal-hole, ribbon and all, but we made every allowance. Moreover, its hair was even more wiry than Mrs. Phinney's, and being very thin its pink skin showed through plainly, in a very chilly and uncomfortable fashion. Still, next to the silhouette of her grandmother, this kitten was little Alice's most precious possession; she soothed its piteous mewings in the same tender voice with which she hushed her dolly's imaginary wailings. With the doll on her knee and kitty curled up in the tiny straw cradle at her feet, Alice sat on the floor perfectly happy, busily engaged in cutting out garments for both to the best of her ability with a large pair of dull scissors whose points were as round as a knife-blade. Often she had to stop and rub the red rings on her poor little thumb and finger, which these cruel scissors made, and often she interrupted herself to burst out in snatches of shrill singing, or to jog the cradle, or to wrap dolly up closer in her small pocket-handkerchief. Little Alice had a genius for loving and nursing.

When Mrs. Phinney was not putting up her hair, she was generally bending over some article of her well-saved wardrobe, darning and repairing it. She would sit mechanically at work hour after hour, her rigid face and compressed lips motionless and expressionless, except of a sort of dull sorrow. I used to sit on the bottom stair, that I might look in upon her and Alice unobserved. Once or twice, to my great astonishment, I saw this marble figure of a woman suddenly drop her work and fall on her knees by the child, kissing her vehemently without a word, and wetting her hair with a shower of tears. Alice would look up with some wonder and more sympathy, speak to her mother in little soothing tones as if she were comforting another doll, and wipe her eyes with whatever odd-shaped frock or pinafore she might be working upon. In a few moments the mother would return to her seat, resume her work listlessly, and her eyes would look as dry and stony as if they did not know how to weep.

We never saw much of Alice. Sometimes she entered our room unobserved, and when we looked up from our play, we found her standing by, hugging the everlasting doll, and watching us with quiet satisfaction. We always were glad to see her and made her immediately useful. She was willing to "make believe" anything, and to be either our visitor or our maid or our child, elder sister of Angelina Augusta or Augusta Angelina; she would keep a baker's, a butcher's, or a greengrocer's shop, whichever we chose, and allowed us to *beat her down* in her prices to our heart's content. But in the midst of our bargaining, Mrs. Phinney's anxious voice would be heard calling "Alice, Alice!" and the child was gone in a moment. "I suppose Mrs. Phinney will not let Alice play with us because she thinks we are furniture-smashers," I said to Anne.

Though Alice seemed the most amiable, the most gentle of children, we were sometimes startled, generally late in the afternoon, by her loud and violent shrieking, as if she were in a perfect paroxysm of passion. We heard a running and hurrying of people down stairs on such occasions, Mrs. Phinney's door was hastily shut, and the screams soon ended as suddenly as they began. We did not understand it at all, and thought Alice must be a very bad child in spite of appearances.

On the next morning, after one of these fits of screaming, Alice glided into the room even more gently than ever. I thought I had never seen her look so deadly pale. "Do you feel ill?" said I to her. "O, no," said she, " only a very little tired ; my doll has been rather troublesome, and I can't make kitty stay in the cradle this morning. I suppose it is lifting her into it so many times which makes me ache so all over. Then the breakfast was not good, the milk was sour, and the bread was very dry, I could not swallow them. Mother says her milkwoman is as good as any, but I wish she'd get another; very often in the morning something ails the milk so that I can't eat my breakfast."

Now it happened that I had been reading some very interesting stories by Mrs. Sherwood, where total depravity was insisted upon, and a great deal said about the ingenuity of men and children in attributing wrong motives to their actions, deceiving themselves as well as others. Here, I thought, was a decided case of depravity and self-deception under my very eyes, and I felt myself called upon to make a missionary effort in Alice's behalf.

"Alice," said I, with considerable sternness, " you were a very naughty girl last night, and you screamed yourself sick. *That* is what makes you so tired today, and that is the reason you could n't eat your breakfast. It is not the fault of the milkwoman nor of the kitten, but of your bad heart," I added sol-

147

emnly, "and you ought to pray to God to forgive you and help you not to do so any more."

Little Alice looked very much astonished.

"I was n't naughty last night," she said gently, "I am *never* naughty."

This seemed to me a very serious case.

"O Alice," I said, "how little you know yourself! your heart is desperately wicked, and you are naughty all the time, even when you 're asleep."

I was almost afraid this was going beyond Mrs. Sherwood, but Alice was in such a hardened condition that I thought it best to state the case strongly.

"If you were me," said Alice, after a moment's silence, "would you put a ruffle on dolly's new night-cap?"

I determined to try an appeal to her feelings, since I could not succeed in convincing her mind.

"O Alice," I cried, "how can you be naughty when you think of your poor mamma! She has nobody in the world left to love her but you. I 've seen her cry over you, and I 've seen her looking as sad as if her heart was breaking. Perhaps it is because you are so bad. If you would try to be good, I dare say she would laugh and — *smile*," I concluded, rather awkwardly; but this time some effect was produced. Two very large tears gathered slowly in Alice's very large eyes, and she looked at me with a wistful and bewildered expression.

"Mamma cries because she says she's afraid she shall lose me," she answered in a troubled voice. "I don't think she can lose me. I always hold her hand so tight when we walk in the streets over at Liverpool, and here there's no danger, for I know the way everywhere as far as the brick church."

I felt my missionary zeal ebbing away very fast as I looked at the poor little pale face.

"I rather think," continued Alice, somewhat reassured, "that mother thinks grandma will find me if I *do* get lost. Last night, when I was falling asleep, she said she believed I should soon follow grandma. I heard her say so to the cook. And so I *shall* follow her, just as soon as I get a glimpse of her, and I mean to look about everywhere for her next time I go to Liverpool. Is Liverpool the way to heaven?"

149

This was so fair an opportunity that I could not help saying, "The way to heaven is to be *good*, Alice, and I 'm sure your mamma would be happier if you were good."

" Well, then, I 'll be good," said Alice.

"That 's right," cried I, delighted with my success, "and, Alice, I 'll show you the beautiful prayer and hymn that Henry Fairchild learned after he had been very naughty. You had better read it."

" I can't read," said Alice, "except d-o-g dog, and h-a-t hat, in the primer."

" Well," said I, " I 'll read them to you."

I began to read, and Alice very soon began to yawn; presently a new idea struck her, she turned towards me quickly, and burst into a fit of laughter. I had never heard her laugh so before.

" Why," said she, " what a stupid thing I am ! you 're only *making believe*. I forgot that you always make me play at *being something* when I come up here. O yes, I know now, I 'm to play I was naughty last night. Well, mother," she said in a funny voice, pretending to cry, "I'm very sorry, please not whip me very hard!"

She held out her little hand for me to strike it, as I often did by way of imaginary punishment, and affected to be very much frightened.

"Please not punish dolly," she said. "Play she was the best of all. Let my dolly wear the medal to-day, if we keep school."

I hung the button which served for a medal round the rag-baby's neck. I was quite puzzled.

Next time that we heard Alice screaming I got up from my cricket, threw Angelina Augusta into Anne's lap, and went in search of Mary. I met her on the stairs; she looked agitated and alarmed. "What is the matter with Alice?" I asked, anxiously.

"Matter, miss?" said Mary; "children does be always screaming; maybe she's naughty."

"No, Mary," said I, "Alice is not naughty."

"Then what can she have to scream for?" retorted Mary, twitching her gown from my grasp and leaving me. I ran to mamma's room.

" Mamma," cried I, " what ails Alice ? why does she shriek so ? "

Mamma hesitated, and replied, " She cries because she does not feel well."

The cries suddenly ceased. " Does she feel better now ? " I asked.

" I hope so," said mamma, still hesitating.

I went behind the window-curtain to ponder on the mystery. The setting sun poured a river of light against the current of the Mersey ; each wave had its spark of fire like an opal. Little boats with glowing sails flew rapidly along, large ships felt their way more cautiously through the glorified atmosphere. Hundreds of fluttering streamers pointed down the river ; they seemed to say to the lagging vessels, " There is your way, there lies the path to the great ocean, beautiful lands with golden gardens and sapphire skies are hidden behind those western clouds ; follow us, from their dizzy mast-heads we shall first discern the splendors beyond." I pitied the ships shut up in the docks, whose pennons streamed eagerly upon the breeze, but in vain. Then

I thought those pent-up masts behind those enormous
walls were like the great trees in Beelzebub's garden;
the little scarlet and crimson flags looked at that
distance like gorgeous diabolical fruit.   Then I
thought of poor Matthew who got such a terrible
pain by eating Beelzebub's apples, and I wondered if
Alice's pain was as bad.   It must be, if one could
judge by her screams.   Mary now entered the room.
She did not see me, and exclaimed to mamma, " O
ma'am, the poor child is in a terrible fit.   The doctor
says she can't live through many more."   I suppose
mamma made a sign to her that I was in the room,
for she immediately began talking of something else.
I had a vague idea that a fit was a dreadful thing.
Giant Despair had fits; there was a picture of him
while " his fits were upon him " in Mrs. Mason's old
" Pilgrim's Progress," — a hideous picture, in which
he sprawled all over the page, kicking and clutch-
ing, with every feature purposely out of drawing,
to represent extreme agony.   A fit was a thing too
shocking to be spoken of, and I went to bed full of
consternation and excitement.

We did not see Alice for several days, and though the weather was very warm, Mrs. Phinney's door was constantly shut. One evening, after a very hot day, mamma gave me leave to go into the garden. I went alone, for Anne was too languid to play. The garden descended rapidly in terraces towards the river, so that from the lowest terrace the house was not visible, only water and sky, the distant city opposite, and a lonely shore stretching away to the right and left. With a good deal of difficulty I turned a large empty flower-pot upside down, and seated myself upon it, under a gnarled apple-tree. I shall never forget that night: the sky was hung with murky clouds, thunder muttered in the distance; the river laughed and danced no more, but rolled sternly and resolutely on to the sea. Liverpool was wrapped in mist, through which glowed a few fiery eyes, peering out at the lightning perhaps, which now and then warmed up the cold gray of earth and sky. The wind rose slowly; it sighed very gently at first, nestled itself against the quivering leaves, and rested there; soon the sighs grew longer and louder, and the wind rushed farther and farther out into the gathering darkness; the sighs became sobs, and the sobs became cries, as if the gale was resolved to outdo the thunder, which growled more and more fiercely. As the storm advanced with more and more swiftness, it suddenly grew very dark; I could not see three feet before me, and though I hardly dared move, I longed to be in the house. Just as I was about to start up and make a desperate rush towards the first flight of steps in my cowardly haste, a broad flash of lightning showed me Alice, standing within reach of my hand. I gave a violent start and scream; she did not appear to hear or see me; her eyes were rolled far back in her head, which was turned towards the sky; her face was as leaden as the clouds. So intense was her attitude, that I felt she saw something that I could not see. I trembled with inexpressible curiosity and dread. In a second it was all blackness again, but Alice's face looked up before the eyes of my imagination as plainly as I had just beheld it in bodily vision. "Alice," said I, "tell me, do you see your grandmother in heaven?"

A frightful shriek was the only answer, another and another, and now the lightning glared continually, and I saw the long figure of Mrs. Phinney flying down the steps, her hair streaming as usual, but this time it seemed awful to me, and not ridiculous. She flung herself upon Alice, or *could* it be Alice, that little white quivering form? The lightning seemed to play in the mother's hair as she toiled up flight after flight, from terrace to terrace, with her woful burden, nor could I tell, in the hurly-burly of the storm, which was thunder, which was wind, which was Alice screaming or her mother groaning. I suppose I got into the house and was put to bed as usual, but I remember nothing about it.

"You are very quiet this morning, miss," said Mary to me at breakfast next day. "Do you know what is going on in the house?"

I remembered to have seen that look and heard that tone before, when Mary had come to tell me my little brother was dead. I did not make any answer, but I knew that Alice was dying or dead. By and by there was a long whispered consultation between mamma, Mary, and Mrs. Phinney's cook, who came up stairs with red eyes. When it ended, mamma said to me very gently, —

"Little Alice is very sick, she will soon be in heaven; her pain has left her, and she will have no more of her terrible spasms. She is very quiet now, and she wants very much to see you. I think you had better go down and bid her good by, for she has been a kind little playmate to you. But be very still, and don't agitate her by crying."

Mary took me by the hand, led me down stairs into Mrs. Phinney's room, and left me at Alice's pillow. Instinctively I first looked at the mother; what was the sorrow of the child's death compared to the future sorrow of that mother's life? Mrs. Phinney's eyes were as stony, her features as rigid, as ever. But her hands were in constant nervous agitation, now smoothing the bedclothes, now arranging the pillows, now wiping the child's brow with her handkerchief. I fixed my eyes at last on Alice. Her hair, tangled, matted, soaked with the sweat of the mortal agony she had endured, was spread all over

the pillow, and against this dark background, so ex-
pressive of suffering, lay the whitest, stillest, sweetest
face in the world.

"Here is Miss Peasy come to see you," said the
mother, speaking in a measured voice, as if afraid to
trust herself.

Alice opened her eyes. How they shone! light
flowed from them. She stirred her little closed hand.
I took it; it felt in my grasp as slight as a withered
flower. A playful expression flitted over her face, as
she whispered to me, —

"I 've been sick, I 've got well now. Mother gave
me some arrowroot, but I could n't drink it; cook
spoiled it. I gave it to Snowball; she ate it out of a
saucer. Only think, cook says Snowball caught a
mouse in the cellar last night! Was n't she a clever
kitten?"

She gave a sigh of exhaustion. Her mother offered
some more arrowroot and lifted her up gently. The
child tried to drink, but was almost strangled in the
attempt to swallow; a faint color flushed her cheeks.
After a few moments she sighed out, "What bad ar-

rowroot! that was *your* fault, cook, but I dare say you could n't help it."

The poor cook, who had lived with Mrs. Phinney for many years, cried bitterly, and covered her head with her coarse apron.

"Mother," whispered Alice, with more strength than seemed possible, "did n't you say I was going to heaven to-day? I can't, I don't feel well enough, and I 'm not dressed. And I can't go without dolly. Give me dolly."

Her mother laid the doll close to the child's face. Alice murmured to it in her usual way, "Pretty dolly, dear dolly, do you love me?" Then the voice died away.

"Something ails me," she said quickly, with a look of terror. "Give me kitty, quick!"

Snowball was rubbing about my feet. I picked her up, and Mrs. Phinney put her on the bed.

"Good mother!" said Alice, making up her mouth to be kissed. Her mother bent over her, and their lips met; the mother's heart went out from her in that kiss, and Alice took it with her to heaven.

She lingered yet a moment, the kitten was licking her hand. The child glanced first at Snowball and then at me; the same playful expression struggled with death in her face, but for an instant only. She laid her cheek against her dolly, as I had seen her do it many times before, the eyelids dropped, and the splendid light of those eyes went out forever.

" Well, dear," said mamma to me after I was taken up stairs, " did you bid Alice farewell? Did she tell you she hoped you would meet her in heaven? did she know she was going to God?"

" If you 'll believe me, ma'am," burst out Mary, " the poor child knew no more about God than a little heathen. Ma'am, she actually died hugging up that dirty rag-doll, just as she used to do when she was at play."

Mamma made no answer. " O Mary!" was all I could say, but I had learned a lesson of death, though I was unable to repeat it. Those are sometimes nearest to God who are most unconscious of it, was what I felt, but could not express.

VI.

THE ISLE OF MAN.

" AND so there they lay," continued papa, " stiff and cold, but with smiles on their little thin faces, and hundreds of robins fluttered over them, showering down leaves upon them, and not only leaves but rose-petals and lily-petals, and thousands of small flowers, violets and periwinkles and wood-anemones, so that very soon these poor babes in the wood grew into a charming green bank covered with bees and butterflies all day long, and their poor dead limbs were sheltered from the rain and sun."

Here papa paused. Deep sobs were heard from two little girls who sat on his knees. One of these little girls saw him through her tears winking at mamma, and pointing out to her the effect he had produced, but it did not make any difference; the babes in the wood were dead just the same whether papa chose to laugh or not.

"And now, Peasy," said papa, "if you will get me your 'Paul and Virginia,' I will read you the chapter which describes the wreck of the Saint Geran and the drowning of Virginia."

"O no, papa," I cried, "you know I can't bear to hear that chapter; you know I can't help running out of the room when you come to that part where it says, 'Virginia placed one hand on her heart and raised her eyes to heaven' — just as she sees the great wave coming. No, papa, I sha'n't get the book; I've hidden it on purpose, and I hope you'll never find it."

"Never mind about the book," said papa. "I know the story pretty well; indeed, I believe I can tell it better than I can read it." He began. "'Paul plunged into the waves with his arms stretched out towards Virginia; Domingo and I held the ends of the rope which we had tied round his waist.'"

"Did you, papa?" said Anne, looking up very respectfully, but I stopped my ears with my hands and sang out loudly, —

"There was a man in our town,
  And robbers came to rob him,
  He crept up to the chimney top,
  And then they thought they had him.
  But he got down on t' other side,
  And then they could n't find him.
  He ran fourteen miles in fifteen days,
  And never looked behind him."

Papa's voice was drowned, and Virginia was saved alive that night. A violent game of romps ensued amid great laughing and shouting, in the midst of which mamma was heard mildly remonstrating, "My dear, you will really disturb the neighbors. O my dear, take care of that lamp. My dear, you'll waken the baby."

At length Anne's pinafore being torn from her shoulders, and my shoe-strings broken short off, there was a cessation of hostilities.

"Peasy," said papa, drawing me towards him, "let's see how much of a scholar you are. Where is Dublin situated, and what is it famous for?"

My wits and breath were quite gone after such a stormy play, but papa should have an answer.

"Dublin," said I, boldly, "is the capital of Ireland; it is situated on the Shannon, and is famous for its Limerick gloves and the Giant's Causeway."

"Peasy," said mamma, gravely, "remember that to-morrow you are to be put back in your geography as far as 'Chapter VII., Ireland.'"

"O mamma," said I, "that's too bad, when I've got away along, as far as the Cannibal Islands."

"No, no," said papa, "I know a better way to teach geography than that. The best method of finding out where Dublin is situated is to go and see for one's self. To-morrow, mother, you may pack up the children's clothes, and next day we'll take the steam-packet Royal George, which sails for Dublin at ten A. M. precisely. I warrant we'll find the Shannon, if it is to be found there, and I dare say Peasy has got money enough to buy herself a pair of the Limerick gloves. Perhaps she can get them cheap at the manufactory."

As mamma did not say as usual, "My dear, what nonsense you are talking!" I went to bed, thinking that papa was very likely to be in earnest, especially as his way of learning geography struck me as extremely sensible and natural. Mamma and Mary *did* spend the whole of the next day in packing, and, moreover, I was *not* put back to "Chapter VII., Ireland." I went through a hurried lesson about the Cannibal Islands over the top of a great trunk which mamma was filling, and upon which she nailed a card of direction with DUBLIN printed at the bottom in very black ink. This was conclusive. Anne and I spent the rest of the day in consulting Robinson Crusoe, whose experience in sea voyages afforded us some valuable hints, and in lingering on the stairs that we might waylay Mrs. Phinney and the cook, and tell them that we were going to Dublin. We wrapped up our dolls in their warmest clothes, and privately tied to their waists broad corks from a couple of empty pickle-jars; we hoped, in case of shipwreck, they might be able to float ashore on these, with perhaps some traces of paint remaining on their faces. On the day of departure we went in our cloth coats and beaver bonnets to bid Mrs. Phinney good by. She looked very sad when she kissed us; we knew she was thinking of Alice, and we were truly sorry for her, but then we were going to Dublin, we could not help being happy. Snowball purred an affectionate farewell; "the way Mrs. Phinney pampered up that cat," Mary said, "was really extraordinary for a sensible middle-aged woman!"

Cook bestowed upon us each a paper of buns and oranges, we were fairly loaded down with baggage, as all travellers ought to be, and what with dolls, buns, and baskets, we went aboard the Royal George as heavily accoutred for our size as Robinson Crusoe with his two muskets, four pair of pistols, powderhorn, hammer, and shot-bag.

Mamma, Mary, and baby disappeared at once down the cabin stairs. The weather was unpleasant, the wind being fresh and the sky cloudy; but, as papa said, "it did not much signify; we should run across in a few hours, and be in Dublin before the storm. The Royal George was an excellent sea-boat, and made her passages very punctually." We stayed on deck with papa, and in obedience to mamma's injunctions we held fast by his hands, and looked about us, we and

i.

the dolls, to our heart's content. We admired everything, even to the muddy river, with the color and
foam of porter; the sand-bars; the buoys, which
would bob up and down as if they were alive, making us hope perpetually that we were coming to a
whale or a seal, in spite of repeated disappointments;
the vessels at anchor, with topsails clewed up like so
many great cradles for the idle sailors, who lay about
the decks and slept to the swinging and rocking of
the tide; the ships beating about under sail, where
the crew were wide awake and bustling, where we saw
little figures of men running and climbing, and heard
the cheery " yo-heave-oh's " crossing each other from
ship to ship on the breeze.

In the midst of all this excitement of course it
was impossible that we should content ourselves with
travelling as two insignificant little girls in beaver
bonnets; we determined to choose distinguished characters for ourselves, and, after due deliberation, we
resolved to be Lady Stamford and Lady Belgrave,
going with our children on a voyage to the Isle of
France,—an island we especially affected for Virginia's

sake. These were two titled ladies whom we had often admired in M......, riding in their coroneted carriages and attended by servants in livery. So we sat down together on a couple of high stools, spread out our dresses in a dignified manner, called one another by our titles as often as possible, and conversed in the most elegant language we could muster. Several gentlemen came up to talk to papa, and for want of something better to do, began to notice us with that condescending familiarity which grown-up men six feet high assume towards children whose heads hardly reach to their elbows.

"Come here, little one," said a stout good-natured-looking man, holding out his hand to me; "bring your rattle-traps over this way, and sit on my knee."

Here was a pretty address to be made to Lady Stamford! My dignity rebelled against it, but nevertheless I felt obliged to obey, and walked slowly across the deck towards the gentleman's knee. The Royal George was pitching considerably, and as I was encumbered with my doll and my basket, I fell down; the basket flew open, and out rolled all the conveniences I had provided for Angelina Augusta's comfort in travelling, — the pewter cup and spoon, two tiny clean pocket-handkerchiefs in case of sickness, a vial supposed to contain salts, a small wooden lemon, and a nightgown.

"Good gracious, child," cried the gentleman, picking up the doll, "how do you manage to lug about all this trumpery?"

He lifted me in a very indignant state upon his knee. That he should call Angelina Augusta *trumpery*, and sit there holding her so contemptuously by the neck!

"What's your name?" said he, abruptly.

No answer. I dared not reply "Lady Stamford," and really just at that time I *was* Lady Stamford and nobody else.

"Where are you going?" he asked, after waiting in vain for me to speak.

No reply again. If I answered at all, I must say "To the Isle of France." In imagination I was already there; in imagination I saw the waters of Virginia's fountain sleeping in the moonlight, and the two

palm-trees whispering together over her "Repose."
I saw the bamboo huts of Madame de la Tour and
Marguerite, and the little white church of the Shad-
dock grove; I saw the town of Port Louis lying between the dark, tangled tropical forest and the broad
blue Indian Sea; I saw the Island of Bourbon in the
distance like a solitary cloud in the unstained sky of
the south.

"I fancy you've left your tongue in Liverpool,"
said the gentleman, taking Angelina by the feet instead of the neck, and holding her head downwards,
so that her pink gauze veil trailed over his muddy
boots.

"Not all of it," I burst out. "I've got enough
left to ask for my doll. Please give her to me; she
is not used to being held so; I'm afraid you'll make
her dizzy."

The gentleman laughed, and handed me the insulted
and discomposed Angelina Augusta, whom I pro-
ceeded to "set to rights" gravely.

"How old are you?" said the gentleman.

"Nearly seven," said I, as impressively as possible.

The gentleman yawned, and, having exhausted his resources in the way of entertaining children, he allowed me to slide from his knee.

As I was returning to Anne, walking as much like Lady Stamford as the motion of the vessel allowed, I was suddenly lifted into the lap of a very pleasant-looking young man who had been sitting very near us, quite near enough probably to overhear our childish talk and be amused by it.

"That is a charming little girl you have with you, ma'am," said he, taking the doll in a very respectful manner. "I hardly ever saw such black eyes in a child of her age. She resembles you extremely," he added gravely, studying both our faces; "you are her mother, I presume?"

"Yes, sir," said I, "she is my only child; her name is Angelina Augusta."

"And a delightfully sweet name you have given her," returned he. "If you will allow me, I will write it down in my pocket-book in case I should ever want to name a daughter of my own."

The pocket-book was brought out, and the name

inscribed in a bold hand with many ornamental flourishes.

"And now, ma'am —" continued he.

"Stop," interrupted I, "you should say 'your ladyship' when you speak to me. I am Lady Stamford."

"Pardon me," he answered seriously, "I was not aware — but believe that I am most happy to make your ladyship's acquaintance."

We shook hands, and bowed to each other politely.

"That is my sister, Lady Belgrave," I continued, pointing to Anne, who had fallen asleep in a little bunch, with her head against the guard. Her bonnet was very much jammed, the front of her coat covered with crumbs of bun, and her mouth stained with orange juice.

"I hope," said he, "your ladyship will take an early opportunity of introducing me to her ladyship, your ladyship's sister."

"What elegant language!" thought I; "now this is the proper way for me to be spoken to."

"Might I inquire of your ladyship," continued

this delightful man, " what point of the compass is, on this voyage, honored with your ladyship's approval? In other words, I would ask your ladyship in which direction your ladyship is going?"

" O, to the Isle of France," I replied. " Virginia and I went to the same convent to school in Paris, and I promised her we would come and stay a week or two with her some time."

" Your ladyship could not do better," returned he. "I am myself a cousin of the governor at Port Louis, M. de la Bourdonnaie; perhaps your ladyship has heard Virginia speak of him?"

" O, very often!" I cried. " He was the person who obliged her to go to Paris, and I hope, sir, you will advise the governor not to make a fuss now that she has concluded to go back and marry Paul."

" I think," said he, "your ladyship had best speak to the governor yourself. I will do my utmost to confirm your ladyship's influence."

There was a pause. How charming this style of conversation was! O, if Lady Belgrave would only wake up and listen to it, — but she was snoring loudly, and papa was wiping her face with a red bandanna pocket-handkerchief.

"I hope we shall not get to the Isle of France in the hurricane season," said I.

"I trust not," answered he, "for the sake of your ladyship, your ladyship's sister, your ladyship's child. But your ladyship must remember that the Saint Geran in which Virginia was wrecked was nothing but a French ship, nothing like as strong, of course, as the English heart of oak which has the honor of conveying your ladyship. And by the by, begging your ladyship's pardon, I do not exactly understand. Here is your ladyship going to see Virginia, and yet Virginia is shipwrecked and drowned."

"O, didn't you know?" said I. "She was not drowned *dead,* she was brought to life again after she was found on the beach. I never read any farther than the shipwreck, because the rest of the book is not true. The person who wrote it was mistaken."

"This information that your ladyship gives me is highly satisfactory," returned my friend. "Per-

mit me to remark that your ladyship's face is
rather smutty, owing to your ladyship's proximity
to the chimney. My poor child," cried he, suddenly changing his tone, " you are very pale, you
are going to be seasick. Let me carry you down
into the cabin to your mamma."

It was true enough. Sundry dreadful qualms
had been seizing me occasionally, and, the Royal
George giving a sudden violent lurch, I was over-
come at last. I forgot my dignity, I forgot my
doll, which slipped from my hands to the deck with
a loud bump. I remember being carried by my new
friend down the cabin stairs, followed by papa with
Lady Belgrave, who cried loudly, and whose bonnet
was in a shapeless heap, knocked over her eyes.

The boat was crowded. Anne and I were laid
in one berth in a little dark state-room; papa
opened the door wide, and placed a carpet-bag
against it, that we might get a breath of such air
as the close cabin afforded. What miserable hours
we passed! The pitching and tossing increased
continually, we rolled over and over, bumping

against the sides of the berth, crying heartily when the spasms of seasickness were coming on, and dozing heavily when they were over, in spite of our uncomfortable position, or rather *want* of position, for we could not keep ourselves in one place a moment. Mamma and Mary had only three-legged stools to sit on; they braced themselves against the wall as well as they could, the baby fretting continually, and no wonder, for mamma was obliged to hold the poor little thing in the most awkward manner, to keep it from being thrown out of her arms. Papa put his head into the door sometimes, bringing with him from the deck such a nice smell of fresh sea-air, and looking so well and so wide awake and so rosy that we wondered at him with all the power of wonder seasickness left in us.

"I've been to dinner," said he on one of these visits. "Peasy, don't you want to get up and see the dishes on the table dancing a country-dance? Down the outside they go, down the middle and back, cross over and right and left. Campbell got a tureen full of gravy all over his straw-colored cassimere vest; young Tom Campbell of Glasgow, he's aboard, — and just as the steward was putting the potatoes before the captain, they were all flung out of the dish, and rattled about the captain's head like big hailstones. Peasy, don't you want some dinner? Capital fried soles, juicy sirloin, gooseberry tart, and cheesecakes. You know you like cheesecakes. Have a cheesecake?"

"O papa!" said I faintly, while an inexpressible disgust stole over me. It made us ill even to see mamma and Mary trying to swallow a little tea at favorable moments.

"Mary," said I solemnly, after papa had gone, "come here a minute, don't tell mamma just yet, but I think I sha' n't live a great while longer."

"Bless me! why not, miss?" said Mary, anxiously.

"Because," sobbed I, with a burst of tears, — "because I've left off liking cheesecakes, and that could n't happen to me unless I was going to die."

"O, that's nothing," answered Mary; "you'll come to your stomach in time, miss."

"Peasy," said Anne's melancholy little voice, "I hope our poor dolls are n't *very* sick."

"O dear, I hope not," sighed I. "Please look at them, Mary, and tell us how they are getting on."

"They 're doing beautifully," said Mary. "They 're taking care of one another in the upper berth. They send their best loves down to you, and please you must not worrit, they say, for they have not even lost their color."

"Mary," said I, "why can't you tie the bottle of salts to Angelina's nose and put her nightgown on?"

"Angelina says she don't want it on," replied Mary, promptly, "and she declares she knows where the smelling-bottle is; she 'll get it herself if she wants it."

"O, very well!" I said, feeling as much relieved as if I had not known that Mary was making all these messages up.

The hours wore on. We dozed, woke up, cried, were sick, and dozed again, over and over. The candles in the cabin blinked and winked, and seemed to be dozing too; there was just enough light to make the darkness look darker and mamma's pale face paler. It seemed as if we had been on board the boat ever since we could remember, and that poor mamma, perched bolt upright on her three-legged stool, was as much a fixture as an idol on its pedestal. Sighs, groans, and lamentations were heard in all directions, and the storm thundered without like a great organ out of tune.

"Anne," said I, "don't you wish you were in the Valley of the Shadow of Death? It would n't be half as dreadful as this. And there sit mamma and Mary in two corners, like Pope and Pagan."

Anne was so weak that she began to laugh, so did I; then we cried again, then we laughed and cried together. Papa came in, buttoned up in his great-coat, with a handkerchief tied over his seal-skin cap and under his chin.

"Wife," said he, "I find we 've been grossly deceived in this boat. It turns out that she 's a miserable leaky old tub, perfectly unseaworthy. The machinery has given out somewhere, and here

179

we are tossing about and making very little headway. The Isle of Man passengers expected to land hours ago, and it's doubtful if we touch there before morning. It blows great guns, Peasy, and if this weather lasts till we get to Dublin, I don't know but we shall get shipwrecked against the Giant's Causeway."

"My dear," said mamma, seized with a new idea, " why can't *we* go ashore at the Isle of Man? You see how sick and uncomfortable we are, and I'm sure it is not safe to remain on board this vessel; as you describe her, we have reason to be very much alarmed, and it seems to me quite our duty to leave her as soon as possible."

"Well, if you say so," said papa; "but you know we started to go to Dublin; do you feel willing to give up Dublin?"

"Why," said mamma, "of the two I really think the Isle of Man the most interesting place to visit. I have had a great curiosity to go there ever since we read 'Peveril of the Peak' aloud together. I think we should enjoy ourselves there very much,

— we could see Peel Castle, Castle Ruskin, Goddard Crooen's Stone, — excellent fresh air for the children too. And we could go on to Dublin whenever we chose."

Papa laughed. "The truth is, mother, you 're a bit of a coward," said he. "But we 'll stop at the Isle of Man; you shall have fair notice when we 're nearing the place; keep as quiet as you can till I tell you it 's time to get ready." Papa went off, and Mary gave a sigh of relief.

"'T is just as you say, ma'am," cried she; "it ain't our duty, noway nor nohow, to stop aboard a boat that 's full of cracks. We are flying in the face of Providence, and the sooner we leave off the better."

Soon after this Anne and I fell into so sound a sleep that it was with great difficulty, when the boat at last reached the Isle of Man, we could be awakened by the joint efforts of papa, mamma, and Mary, who shook us, lifted us up, and called to us to "make haste — must dress in a minute — Isle of Man — go ashore at once." We were dragged out of the berth, faint, dizzy, and stupefied. Daylight had struggled into the cabin and made it look cold and gray; we shivered all over. Ladies and gentlemen, cloaked and shawled, with baskets and boxes in their hands, stood about our state-room door, all ready to land. "Hurry, hurry!" cried papa, trying to assist us. He put on our pelisses hind side before, crowded my feet into Anne's shoes, bent her bonnet into polyangles, and then, looking at it very complacently, pronounced it emphatically "straightened for the first time in a proper manner," and concluded by combing my tangled hair in such haste that I cried with the pain.

"There, there, never mind, don't cry!" said he. "We'll go upon deck and take a peep at that mermaid sitting on a rock; she's got her looking-glass hung on a rusty nail, and she's combing her hair for breakfast. *She* don't cry, and her hair is in a great deal more of a snarl than yours."

What *could* be the matter with me? I had lost my taste for mermaids as well as cheesecakes, and did not feel a bit of curiosity about this one. The baby had on so many shawls that nobody but papa could carry it. Mary took Anne in her arms, and mamma led me and Angelina Augusta. For the first time I was conscious that this precious creature was heavy; I could hardly walk across the cabin, and dragged one foot after the other painfully up the companion-way. But no sooner had I stepped upon deck than I felt as light as the

> "old woman of Ealing,
> Who jumped up as high as the ceiling,"

and could have outleaped Malvina Hixon herself. For the first time in my life I saw *the sky* in a great sweep of three quarters of a circle, the fourth being broken by the rocky island under whose lee we were lying. The rain had ceased, the last detachments of storm-clouds were crowding one another over the horizon, and the royal sun, just risen, shot after them innumerable darts of golden rays. The wind had gone down, and the waves, so long driven before it, and now suddenly free from its control, ran eagerly hither and thither, tumultuously lifting up their heads, as if they knew not where to go. The sea was one heaving confusion of dazzling lights, in the level rays of early sunshine.

Then the fresh bracing air had such a heroic quality; all our courage and strength came back to us as soon as we felt it blowing in our faces, and my little sister and I struck up a shrill duet, "Ye Mariners of England," at the top of our small lungs, till mamma begged us not to be so noisy. Then I began looking for the mermaid which papa had just seen, but alas! she was gone. Either she was hiding behind a rock, or else she had gone below after combing the snarls out of her hair. I gazed into the water, hoping to catch sight at least of the last whisk of her tail, when — behold a sudden revelation! I was looking down upon what appeared to be the remains of a drowned city, big roots and stones heaped together in chaotic confusion, and reflecting colors as rich and variegated as if the tiny plants, mosses, and lichens which love to creep over old ruins still clung to them. A delicate swaying motion seemed to pass over those bright surfaces, caused by the glimmering of the water, which added to the deception.

I quite lost myself gazing down into the transparent sea, as I mechanically followed my mother out upon the gang-plank, where the crowd of passengers delayed us a moment. Suddenly I started and shuddered; a dead face, ghastly pale, seemed to be looking up into mine; it was only a white stone dimly visible under the water. I recovered myself in a moment, but it was too late, — I had slipped over the gang-plank in my consternation; and if my mother had not instinctively tightened the grasp of her hand, which, fortunately for me, I was holding, there would *really* have been a little dead face lying among the dark rocks under the shallow sea. I came sufficiently near to being drowned or crushed to frighten my mother horribly, and entitle me to a severe scolding, which I richly deserved, though I was shivering so violently with excitement that I could hardly bring out the necessary words of penitence for my carelessness. The only landing was by a rude staircase cut in the perpendicular wall of rock. I thought it the finest staircase I had ever seen, with its rich shining gray and green and purple tints, its tiny glittering pools of water in its hollows, and its spangles of mica.

"Papa," said I, as we clambered up the steps, "this reminds me of the Loadstone Island where Sindbad the Sailor was shipwrecked. Don't you remember how he scrambled over rough stones till he got to the top, and there he found the temple and the great iron horse that he shot at with an arrow and it fell into the sea?"

"Should n't wonder if this was the very spot," said papa, as we stepped upon the long, solitary pier, one end of which rested on the staircase, "especially," continued he, looking about him, "as there is not an animal of any description in sight. It was very thoughtless in Sindbad to shoot the only horse in the place. I wonder how he supposed I was to get three children and six trunks to the public house."

However, we got there at last, and Anne and I were put to bed on four chairs in a room as small and dark as the cabin we had just left, while papa and mamma went to look for lodgings. The name of the town where we had landed was Douglas, and it was dirty enough to be called Black Douglas.

One afternoon, about a week from this time, Anne and I were sitting on the broad stone step of a manse farmhouse. The country around was bleak and desolate; a few stunted twisted trees were scattered here and there, much like corkscrews stuck in the ground. There were no hedges, no orchards, no waving cornfields, no singing birds. There was no life and motion in the landscape save the rushing of the restless sea, no sound but the sullen boom, boom, of the waves, breaking forever on the savage coast. The Isle of Man was only a morsel in the jaws of the ocean; we felt that only through its forbearance we escaped being swallowed up. We could not forget for a moment that we were still at sea, only on a broader and firmer deck. The atmosphere was full of a luminous mist, golden by day, silver by night, for the moon was near her full. Papa and mamma had gone to walk to the top of a barren hill near by, "and," said Mary, "if it was not for this fog, we should see them plainly from here when they get to the top, looking about as slim and black up against the sky as number eight needles."

Mamma was determined to prove that curiosity to see the place, and nothing else, had induced her to stop at the Isle of Man. She explored in every direction till she was brought up by the sea, with "Peveril of the Peak" and a guide-book in her hand. She had taken me to an old ruined castle, nodding over the surf and sinking by degrees into its white arms. She had taken me also to Holm-Peel, another castle formerly of immense strength; its great hall was still used as a prison, the walls and ceiling and floor being of solid stone several feet thick; we felt, on entering it, as if going into a cave. I had a terrible idea of criminals, and I went in among them with fear and trembling, holding fast to mamma's gown.

"Good for nothing wretches!" said papa.

"Poor creatures!" sighed mamma.

"What did you think of the prisoners?" said Anne to me when we got back; "were you afraid to go in?"

"Why, Anne, there is n't the least thing to be afraid of," said I. "It felt so strange not to be frightened, especially as they had n't any fetters on. You know we thought they'd be sitting in a row with their feet and hands tied, but they looked just like other folks. *You* might have gone just as well as not. One man wanted to shake hands with me, only he had warts. They were not punished a bit while we were there, only one of them was reading a sermon. One man was very nice-looking; he said, 'What a pretty little girl!' when he looked at me; he was really as handsome as papa. One old man sat staring at the floor, and I thought he'd dropped a pin. The ugliest creature in the room gave me some sugar-plums."

"That was the turnkey," said mamma; "prisoners never have candy to give away."

"O yes, so he must have been, for he had a pocket-handkerchief, but it was so snuffy! And *such* a pimple on his nose! O mamma, I do so wish I might go again, and carry a sixpence for that *good, good* prisoner, — the one, mamma, that told you he was a sinful wretch, and that God was very good to punish him. Well, he whispered to me afterwards, and asked me 'if I had ever a six-pence about me.' And I told him I had n't any pocket, because my handkerchief was pinned to my belt, but if I had happened to have a sixpence tied up in a corner of it, I would have given it to him."

* * * * *

"Mamma," said I one day coming to her parlor after a long conference with the landlady, — "mamma, I have learned something that will be very useful for you to know, — that people ought to set pans of milk on their kitchen hearths every night for the fairies; Mrs. Cubbins, our landlady you know, always does. They drink it all up before morning. She says she has often come down stairs softly in the night and heard them supping it up, but they have such wonderful sharp ears, she can't move softly enough to catch them, off they scamper when they hear her coming. They wear little slippers made of acorns, and they go pattering over the floor— Oh! and she says they pay for the milk by keeping the kitchen chimney from smoking and the soot from tumbling down and the cream from souring. Do let Betty save milk for the fairies when we go back to M...... Don't you remember how the soot fell once right into the crown of her clean cap as she was stooping over the fire, and how angry she was? Was not it funny what she said? 'By the bare bones of me old grandmother.'"

"Peasy," said mamma, gently, "don't repeat Betty's sayings. And surely you don't believe in fairies?"

"Why," said I, hesitating, " perhaps there are not many left in England, though there must have been plenty formerly. You know one of my best stories begins 'Once on a time when fairies inhabited the earth!' And I am sure there must be a great many in the Isle of Man, they could n't very well get away after they once came, you know. Mrs. Cubbins says she don't think they know how to swim. She sees them sometimes at a distance when she is out walking; they wear green turbans, and wave green flags by the side of the road. Once she met a fairy in the shape of a black pig, and next day her daughter sent her some sausages; another time she heard a great moo-oo-ing all round her as she was walking in the twilight, and in less than a year after, her son in Douglas made her a present of a cow. They always appear to her 'as an omen of good,' she says, on account of the milk she gives them. But they dragged her brother-in-law's wooden leg into the fire one night, and it was found turned to charcoal next morning. And she knows an old man who had all the hair in his best wig pulled out by fairies, — I suppose to make their nests with; but Tom Cubbins always laughs when his mother speaks of it, and says, " Rats, ma'am, rats."

" Yes," interrupted little Anne, " and papa read

to mamma last night, 'Rats and mice are such small _dears,_' but _I_ don't like 'em!"

Here mamma laughed very much, and said, "I must not forget to tell papa that."

"And when Tom laughs," I went on, "his mother is afraid, and she speaks quite low, and looks about her, and says, Don't laugh at the good people, Tom, or some harm will come to you."

"Peasy," said mamma, "go and get your Roman history; you are wasting your time shockingly, and you really _must_ attend to your lessons. To-day you read about Horatius Coccles."

But I have wandered away from Mrs. Cubbins's doorstep, where Anne and I were sitting on a certain summer afternoon. From time to time we looked away from the gray sea, streaked with spray, that we saw dimly rolling under the mist, into the great kitchen, where the strong clear light of the fire was reflected from rows of pewter platters, and from the oaken buffet and settles and the well-scrubbed dresser. The floor was strewn with glittering sea-sand: the baby's frock was no whiter; it touched the floor as Mary sat in a rush-bottomed rocking-chair, hushing it to sleep. The little creature answered with a drowsy murmur, and the spinning-wheel hummed under Mrs. Cubbins's busy hands. Mary, baby, and spinning-wheel droned together, and without the waters moaned; Mrs. Cubbins's large gray eyes had a dreamy, hazy look that must have been caught from the sea.

Tom Cubbins came whistling round the corner from the stable, with a basket in his hand, which he set down before us.

"I thought you 'd maybe like to play with our cat and her kittens," said he, "so I 've brought 'em up to the house. Puss keeps her kittens in the stable, and she don't allow herself time to come up to the kitchen for food, she 's so anxious about 'em. Sometimes I steal some of the fairies' milk off the hearth for her, and I don't believe they miss it."

What did it mean? There they lay, — old puss and one, two, three kittens, — and not one of them — could it be possible? yes, it was certainly so — not *one* of them had — a tail!

"Tom," said I, indignantly, "this is a great deal worse than laughing at the fairies, — I had no idea you were so wicked! How *could* you do so?"

"Do what?" said Tom, looking astonished.

"Don't pretend you *did n't*," said I, "don't deny it. How *could* you cut off all those dear little tails? What did you want them for?"

Tom burst out laughing. "Our Manx-cats have no tails," said he. "I forgot you did n't know it."

Here was an interesting fact. Anne and I selected the two prettiest kittens to nurse, and examined them attentively.

"Puss looks sorry," said Anne, "because she can't lend the kittens a tail to play with."

And indeed the whole family had a resigned look, as though they were trying to submit to the loss of their natural playthings.

"*Four* cats, instead of *two*, must have walked into the ark," I mused, as I slowly stroked my kitten, each stroke coming to an abrupt and unnatural termination, — "two with their tails straight up in the air, and two of this kind, that did n't get finished off."

"How did it happen?" I added, looking up to Tom, who was gazing eagerly down the road.

"Halloo, mother," he cried without answering me, "here is Master Fleetwood coming, I do believe. I see the post-chaise. Got his room ready?"

"But about the cats' tails?" I urged, catching him round the leg, as he was rushing away to meet the chaise.

"Cats' tails?" he repeated. "O, I don't know,— never asked, never heard." Then, taking pity on my anxious face, he added hurriedly, "Ask *him* when he comes, ask Master Fleetwood,— he has lived here all his life, and he knows everything besides; *he*'ll tell you."

And off he went at full speed.

Anne and I settled ourselves to take a good stare at this approaching prodigy, Master Fleetwood, who knew everything; but we were deprived of the pleasure by Mary, who, having disposed of the baby, suddenly appeared on the threshold of the door, and ordered us into the house.

"And you ought to be ashamed," said she, as she

propelled us vigorously up-stairs before her, "to sit there blocking up the doorway when a stranger is coming, — Master Fleetwood too, such a nice boy Mrs. Cubbins says he is, and his grandfather is *Deemster* of the island, besides."

As we crossed the staircase window, on our way to our rooms, we had a glimpse of Master Fleetwood taking a flying leap from a post-chaise which was just drawing up at the front gate, and of Mrs. Cubbins, with fluttering cap-strings, running to meet him.

Anne and I agreed that we would get acquainted with him as soon as possible, that we might ask the great question about the Manx-cats' tails.

"Not that I believe he knows everything, as Tom says," I observed to Anne; "how can he, when his grandfather is only a *teamster?*"

"The Teamster of the island, she *said*," answered Anne. "So I suppose he gets all the work and all the wages."

Unluckily we did not find it very easy to get acquainted with Master Fleetwood, — a long-armed,

197

long-legged youth, in our eyes a man, who spent all
his days in out-door amusements, and was never in
the house, save at meal-times, which he attended with
a punctuality that won Mary's heart; she was never
weary of holding him up as an example to us, careless
little things who never were ready for dinner.

"Why can't you come in when you smell the dinner, as Master Fleetwood does?" she would say,
scrubbing our faces and hands with might and main,
and keeping one eye on the clock, which was on the
stroke of dinner-time. "I declare to Moses, I can't
get off this pigsty mud, — O, *what* children!"

When Mary was very much *put out* with us, she
always "declared" it to somebody. It was not always "to Moses"; she often "declared to Jacob"
or "Jerusalem" or "Abraham," but she never did
it unless we were really *too* trying.

"But we did n't smell the dinner," I answered,
as well as I could, with my mouth full of suds; "we
only smelt the pigsty."

"I should think so, indeed," said Mary, indignantly.
"Well, when the big hog has eat up Miss Anne,

you 'll wish you 'd been good children, and come in regular to your breakfasses and dinners, instead of making me hunt the very shoes off my feet before I 'd find you ; I declare to Samson, you will ! "

Little Anne ventured to steal a respectful look at Mary's feet, which were, however, cased in strong leather shoes, having what she called " a sixpence worth of *squeak* in 'em " ; but indeed Mary might well be vexed with us. After a long search she had found us, just before dinner, at the back of the pig-sty, I holding Anne by the legs, while she hung over the fence, almost within reach of the hog's snout, and fed that interesting animal with clover.

Master Fleetwood's appetite at table inspired us with great respect; we used to forget to eat ourselves, and let the bread and milk drip out of our spoons upon our bibs, while we watched him devouring boiled beef, stewed cow-heel, bubble-and-squeak (cabbage and pork, cooked together), and other farmer's delicacies, which he seasoned with so much mustard and horse-radish as made us study his face curiously. But though he sometimes turned very red, and tears would rush suddenly from his eyes, he never allowed himself to cool his burning mouth with water.

At last, on a certain very rainy day, Master Fleetwood condescended to join us in the back attic, where we had been sent to play, among our empty trunks and boxes that had been put there after the unpacking. I was keeping school for Anne, teaching her to count and "add up" by means of certain rows of brass-headed nails which adorned my father's travelling trunk. I had printed for her benefit Rewards of Merit on the backs of old letters; these were

| Perfect. | Good. | Pretty Good. | Bad. |

and I blended amusement with instruction, for after every effort in mathematics I jumped little Anne off the trunk as a reward, and in strict accordance with her merits. If she had been "Perfect," she was entitled to six jumps; if "Good," to four; if "Pretty Good," to two; and if "Bad," which very seldom happened, to one jump, but it was a *splendid* jump, by way of soothing her wounded feelings.

Master Fleetwood thought this an excellent play, and I remember we soon lost our awe of him. We literally *jumped* into his acquaintance. He amused himself by giving us, in turn, the most superb flying leaps from the top of the trunk that we had ever enjoyed in our lives. We whizzed through the air like flashes of lightning, and he gave us such an impetus that if it had not been for the walls of the attic, I thought we might have soared away, like birds. But Master Fleetwood tired at last of this violent exercise, and flung himself down to rest on Mary's blue wooden box, wiping his face on a handkerchief rather the worse for wear.

"Dear me!" said I, in some concern, "your face is as red as it was yesterday, when you ate so much fresh mustard."

By this time we were so familiar with him that we allowed him to take us one on each knee, as he sat recovering his breath on the box, and I felt bold enough to propound my *great question*.

"Master Fleetwood," said I, "would you be so very kind as to tell us why the cats on the Isle of Man have no tails?"

"Halloo!" said he, "there's a question that never was asked in *my* Natural History. How on earth should *I* know?" Then seeing me look disappointed, I suppose, he added, after a moment's pause, "Probably it happened in the old way."

"Yes," said I, joyfully, "probably it did. But what *was* the old way?"

"Well," he answered, "you 've read of such things in your story-books. By the way, you 've found out, since you 've been here, how much the fairies and such creatures have to do with everything that happens hereabouts on our island?"

"O yes," said I, eagerly, and I was going to repeat several anecdotes in proof of it that I had heard from Mrs. Cubbins, when Master Fleetwood stopped me by assuring me that he knew them all by heart.

"But," said he, "in old times stranger things happened than can occur now, and you may imagine it was a *very* strange thing that made our Manx-cats lose their tails, particularly when I tell you that in the *real* old times of all they had monstrous tails, not a bit like the shrivelled-up things that cats have now in the place where *you* come from; tails no bigger round than your curling-stick — O yes, I 've seen Mary brushing your hair round it many a time, and heard you cry and fret about it, too. No," continued Master Fleetwood, warming with his subject, " the Manx cats that lived once upon a time had great bushy tails like foxes or gray squirrels, — O, they were beautiful, and all the cats admired themselves very much, and took heaps of comfort out of their feathery tails, till one of their royal family took it into her silly head to — to — " Master Fleetwood seemed to be trying to remember the particulars — " yes, that was it, she took it into her head to fall in love with a *prince,* a man-prince with two legs, instead of a cat-prince with four, whom her papa wanted her to marry. No cat was ever prouder of a tail than *she* was of *hers.* It was snow-white, like herself, — you know in your story-books the high-

toned cats are always fair-complected, as Mary says,
—and it curled gracefully at the tip. When she was
in a haughty mood, she used to let it drag after her,
on the ground, like a train. When she felt coquet-
tish, she used to catch it up from the ground, and
carry it under her forepaw, so that she could cast
down her eyes and play with the feathery tip; and
when she wanted to take a walk, she would tie it up
against her waist with her blue sash, so as to be out
of the way."

Here Master Fleetwood paused, apparently to re-
call what came next, and I took the opportunity of
shutting my eyes, and making a picture to myself of
the cat, moving lightly along the dark wood-paths,
appearing and disappearing among the bushes like a
little wreath of cloud or mist; perhaps curling herself up for a nap, when she grew tired, like a big
snow-ball just fallen upon the green grass.

" But what was her name ? " asked Anne.

" Her name," answered Tom, considering, " was
Moi-meme, the princess Moi-meme, for, you see, she
was one of the most selfish little beasts that ever

lived. She never could count further than number *one*. Till she met the prince, and fell in love,
she cared for nobody in the world but her own
precious self; she admired herself so much that she
really pitied people who had n't a chance to wait
upon her and be her servants; she looked at herself
all day in the glass, and dreamed about herself all
night. Even in church, when the clergyman was
preaching, she was always thinking of herself, and so
she never remembered the text."

"How was her name spelled?" I inquired. "I
don't remember seeing it at the end of my spelling-
book; that is where we look when we want new
names for our dolls, or when we play ' ladies '; the
man that wrote the spelling-book. put two pages of
proper names there, and it was real good of him too,
was n't it, Anne? Some of the names are perfectly
splendid."

"O, never mind the spelling!" said Master Fleetwood. "You 'll never find it, it 's not an English
name; just get the pronunciation, that 's all you want,
— Meaw-meme or Miau-meme, that 's about it,—and

a very good name for her it was; it sounded just like her, too, for when she was crosser than usual, and that was almost always, she just miaued and miaued, and spit and yelled, till everybody was tired of her. At the time she first saw the prince, she was not at home; her papa, the old king, had got so weary of her selfish ways that he sent her to stop with a couple of old parties, very wise and excellent old souls they were, too, and the princess Miau-meme used to call them uncle and aunt,— Uncle Wizard and Aunt Witch, those were their names. They had a great deal of patience with her, and so had her papa, because she had no mother; the queen died before the poor princess had got her eyes open, and so she never had been well trained, you see, —spanked, and had her ears boxed, and that kind of thing. Mothers," continued Master Fleetwood, looking seriously first at Anne and then at me, and shaking his forefinger at us slowly, — " mothers are things that we can't any of us very well do without, they are our best friends, don't you know,—first chop, A 1, tip-top sawyers, and that, and they get the upper hands of us when we're small, and they keep it up, whipping us, and putting us to bed without our supper, and so forth, and so on, till we get used to being good, and it comes as easy as winkin'. I don't mind saying," Master Fleetwood continued magnanimously, "that I was a troublesome lot when I was a small chap like you, but my mother never spoiled me by sparing the rod, and *now* you see what a jolly good fellow I've turned out! So take your punishments without making any wry faces, you little shavers, and you'll come out all right. Well, I believe it's going to clear up by noon, and so I must hurry on with my story, for I can't stop in this beastly house all day, if I can help it. So, as I was saying, this disagreeable princess Miau-meme was leading Aunt Witch and Uncle Wizard the very deuce of a life with her tempers and selfishness ; and one rainy day, in particular, she'd been worse than usual, — stopping at home, for you know cats hate water, and cutting up high jinks. Of course she began by licking up all the cream in the pantry that poor Aunt Witch had put by for her tea, and then — she set to work to

catch a mouse. That was all very right for a *cat*, you
know, and it was one of the things she was taught
to do properly at school. Aunt Witch saw her
crouching down behind the ash-bin in the shed,
watching at a mouse-hole, and the good old lady
patted her on the head with her trembling hand, and
praised her for being useful. ' Now is n't it better,'
said she, ' to sit quietly down to some pretty lady-
like work like that, than to be climbing trees, and
clattering over the roof of the house, till my poor
head aches fit to split — like a tom-boy ' — *cat*, I
mean," said Master Fleetwood, correcting himself.
" Well, the princess caught a mouse at last, and
what do you think she did with it ? Why, she
stuffed it into Uncle Wizard's pipe, so it would n't
draw, and she sat under the table and chuckled to
herself when she saw the poor purblind old man
lay his pipe down with a sigh, after trying in vain to
smoke it. ' Well,' says he to himself, ' I must get
my missus to clean out my pipe, and I may as well
put it away now, and go to work and copy off that
receipt for charming away warts,' for he was a Wizard,

you see. So he got up with a groan, for he was a rheumaticky old gent; and he got out his pen and ink, and spread a sheet of paper before him. 'I'll rule it, let *me* rule your paper for you, Uncle Wizard,' calls out Miau-meme, skipping out from under the table. 'That's a nice obliging girl,' says Uncle Wizard, looking at her with some surprise, for she was n't used to wait on him at all, being a princess; the boot was on t' other leg, you know. So she took the ruler, and ruled lines all down the sheet of paper with her little sharp claw, and they were as nice and even as a copy-book. But lo and behold, she had cut 'em clean through the paper, and when Uncle Wizard took it up, the sheet fell apart into twenty ribands, which fluttered down, and settled all over him. But the princess was gone before Uncle Wizard could turn his stiff neck to look after her reproachfully, and as the rain had stopped, off she ran to the brook in great glee, to hunt for white pebbles on the edge of it, with which she meant to fill up the sugar-bowl, after she had stolen out the lumps of sugar for her own eating.

"Well, I can't stop to tell you of her tricks; she had worked all day so hard at being naughty, that she went to bed very early, all tired out. But the rain and wind, that had lulled in the middle of the day, came on in the evening worse than ever, and the princess found she could not sleep, there was such a cracking of branches, banging of shutters, and shaking of windows. She began to feel afraid in all the hullabaloo of the storm, and she called Aunt Witch, in a very rough voice, to come and open her bedroom door, that she might just take a look at the fire for company; her room was next the kitchen, and the kitchen fireplace was in plain sight from her bed. Uncle Wizard and Aunt Witch were dozing over the hearth, for they did not like to go to bed in such a storm, and the princess lay watching their shadows on the wall where their heads seemed to nod from the ceiling down, down, down, till they touched the floor. She thought of a nice trick she could play them; she would pin Aunt Witch's apron to Uncle Wizard's trousers, and then pinch herself to keep awake till they should get up from their chairs to go

to their bedroom. She was just groping her way to
her bureau, that she might get some pins from her
pin-cushion, when she was startled by hearing a
human voice near the house calling for help, and she
had hardly whisked back to her bed, before there was
a knocking at the door, and a voice crying, 'Open,
open, good people, and let me in out of the storm.'
Uncle Wizard was deaf, to be sure, but he was so
kind-hearted that he could always hear a voice in
distress. He was opening the door in a moment, in
spite of his rheumatism, and in rushed not only such
a blast of wind, but such a handsome young prince,
soaking wet, to be sure, yet his cheeks glowed, and his
eyes shone through the water that dripped from his
lovely curling hair. Aunt Witch heaped more wood
on the fire, and the princess could see him well, as he
knelt down in the light of the blaze, after throwing
off his cloak and hat. Little did he think that the
princess Miau-meme was falling deeper and deeper in
love with him every minute, as he drew his long light
curls out between his white fingers to dry them, and
smiled so sweetly on the old couple before him, with

such merry eyes and such shining white teeth. He was all right in a short time, and the princess thought she had never heard music so delightful as his voice, when he related his adventures to the old folks, and told them how he had lost his way in the storm, and got separated from his retinue, as he was returning through the woods to his father's palace."

Here a broad ray of sunshine darted into the room, and Master Fleetwood jumped up as suddenly as if it had pierced him like a spear. " Hulloo, here's fine weather again!" he cried, "and I must go. I'll tell you the rest some other time. Just remember where we left off, you know; prince drying himself, and the princess Miau-meme staring at him. A cat may look upon a king —"

And off he was running, but little Anne seized one hand and I the other, and we begged and entreated him not to go till he had finished the story. " We never, *never* shall hear the end of it unless you tell it to us *now*," I said, " for you know you always lie by the kitchen fire on the settle, and snore all the evening, and besides we go to bed so very early, and perhaps we sha'n't have another lovely rainy day like this — "

" I'm sure I hope not," said Master Fleetwood, fervently.

" And you know you never *have* stayed in the house *once* when the weather was pleasant, — never, — only that one day when you eat too much Sally Lunn, and the other day when you had the brown paper and vinegar on your head, because the bedpost knocked against you."

Master Fleetwood was good-natured ; he hesitated. " Will you tease Mrs. Cubbins to have Sally Lunn for supper, if I'll finish the story ? " he asked.

Of course we joyfully agreed to this, and as the sunshine very opportunely " went in " again as suddenly as it had popped out, he yielded to our wishes, and set himself down once more on the blue box, with the sigh of a martyr. " But I shall hurry up the story as fast as I can," he said, " for when the sun really comes out to stay, you don't catch me wasting my time in the house. Well, it seems the prince was as good a fellow as ever lived, naturally, and he'd been to Sunday school and learned about loving his neighbor as himself, and if it had kept on raining I was going to tell you all the kind things he did for Uncle and Aunt W., on that stormy night when he took refuge in their house, and all the nice speeches he made to them about gratitude and hospitality, and that. Why, besides getting wood and building up the fire, and filling the kettle for tea, and carving the venison pasty with his own hunting-knife, he insisted on carrying the warming-pan for Aunt W., who was trotting about with it, and talking about 'damp sheets.' You see she was making up her own bed for the prince, with clean linen sheets, smelling ever so sweet with lavender; but when he found out it was the only bed in the house, he would n't take it, but just insisted on sitting up over the fire all night. And Princess Miau-meme kept still as a mouse, and watched him as if *he* had been a mouse, too, and admired his good-nature and his good looks with all her silly little heart. Not that she wanted to take to goodness too, and try to be like him; O no, she only

214

wished he would wait upon *her*, and speak kindly to *her*, and smile upon *her*, and she said to herself, ' It 's just my luck to be gone to bed and out of the way on this night of all others, and just like Aunt Witch to be putting herself forward and getting noticed in my place.'

" But at last she dropped asleep, — just, too, as she was wondering what made her so wide-awake, — and slept so soundly, that she did not hear the prince's servants, who had found out where he was, knocking him up early in the morning. To be sure, the prince opened the window softly and forbade their making a noise, as soon as he heard them outside ; and crept out on tiptoe, shutting the door quietly after him, so that the old folks might not be disturbed. The princess was awakened at last by the melancholy sound of Aunt Witch's coffee-mill, which always creaked dismally when she was grinding the coffee for breakfast.

" Well, after that time, the princess, with her usual selfishness, gave herself up entirely to thinking about the prince, and to prowling about in the woods or about the palace, or wherever she could get a chance to peep at him. And wherever she went she overheard the servitors and the cottagers and the huntsmen of the prince forever talking about his goodness and kindness, and how he had done this, that, and the other generous thing for his people. And the princess began to think she should like to do something for *him*, who was so good to every one else; and with her usual unreasonableness, she let this idea take hold of her and grow and grow, till at last she felt not only that she should *like* to do something for the prince, but that she *must* do something for him or die, and finally that it must be a *something* that should tax the very utmost of her power to perform.

" But all this time, she did not forget her beautiful feathery tail, and indeed it was the only thing that gave her any comfort. She was never tired of combing and curling it, of admiring its silvery tip, as it closed itself softly over her paw, or of blowing the fine white hair gently with her breath till it was fluffy and round as a ball. You see she had been flattered for her beautiful tail from the time she was a kitten, just as some children are flattered for their beautiful hair," Master Fleetwood added, significantly looking at my elf-locks, which Mary patiently put into curl-papers every night, in the hope, daily disappointed, that a lovely row of ringlets would reward her for her trouble.   Ah, those curl-papers! they were so tightly twisted at the back of my neck that I seemed to go to bed with a necklace of *prickles*.   Just at the moment Master Fleetwood spoke, I fear my hair was in a more disreputable condition than ever, owing to the dampness of the day, which must have been fatal to curls, and I looked up into his face to see if he could possibly be in earnest in approving of it; I should have been so glad to believe this, but I had an uncomfortable feeling that he was "chaffing," though his face was perfectly sober.   So I tried hard to appear as if I had not considered his remark personal.   "Sometimes," Master Fleetwood continued, going on with his story, — "sometimes it really seemed as if Miau-meme thought as much of her own beautiful tail as she did of the prince. — There's the sun again!"

And up he started. " O dear, — well, it seems to me I never *shall* get through with this story, — you must n't mind my hurrying it along," he added, beginning to speak very fast, and sitting down once more reluctantly. " Well, the princess got into a way of hiding about in the woods, and following the prince whenever he went hunting or riding horseback; she had a sort of an idea that perhaps something would happen to him unexpectedly, and that she might be able to assist him; and O, how delightful it would be, she thought, if she could really do him such a good turn that he *must* feel grateful to her, and she used to shut her pretty green eyes, and fancy the prince smiling at her and speaking to her so gently and kindly.

" Well, at last it was announced that the prince was to have a great hawking-party, the first of the season, in order to try some new falcons that had been sent from England, and that his falconers had been training for a long time. — Now," said Master Fleetwood, stopping short and looking at me severely, " don't you fidget so, and look as if you were going to interrupt me. I know what you are going to say; you are going to tell me you don't know what a hawking-party is, nor what sort of creatures falcons are, and all that, but I can't possibly stop to tell you." Then, thinking I was about to speak, Master Fleetwood put his hand over my mouth. " Hold on!" said he, " I take it all back about the hawking-party, it was a *hunting*-party that was to come off, after all, and I don't know why I made such a mistake, — yes, a hunting-party, to try a lot of new hounds; you know all about that — Well — "

I was very indignant that Master Fleetwood should take me for such an ignoramus, and as soon as I could push his hand away from my mouth, I started up, red as fire, exclaiming, " I know as much about hawks and falcons as *you* do. I had n't the least idea of asking you a single question about them. I read all about hawking-parties long ago, in my father's Strutt — " *

" There, there, there," said Master Fleetwood, soothingly, — " that 'll do. Don't get angry; you

---

* A charming book called "Strutt's Sports and Pastimes."

're as red as a turkey-cock. Your father's Strutt indeed! You look a great deal more like strutting yourself. How should I know you were a Solomon in pinafores? Have a peppermint?" he added politely, producing some pink and white fragments of that sweetmeat from the bottom of his pocket, mixed up with a handful of tacks and ha'pennies, and a common-sized piece of chalk. I was mollified, and, selecting the cleanest morsel of peppermint from among this assortment of treasures, which Master Fleetwood held out to me in his large palm, I ventured to put the question that really *had* been on my tongue's end for some minutes.

"I *did* want to know," I said, "what had become of the *woods* you are talking about so much, for there is n't a tree to be seen now. When you told us there was to be a hawking-party, it reminded me that I had n't asked you that question."

"O, well, I can tell you that in a jiffy," said Master Fleetwood. "You see, when all the fairies left the island, they pulled the trees up by the roots to make rafts of them to cross the water with. And now

I 'll finish the story; there *was* a hawking-party after
all, — I was right at first, — and of course the poor
little pussy-princess was scampering about the county,
here and there and everywhere, climbing up trees and
hiding behind rocks, following the prince as he gal-
loped along, turning and twisting this way and that,
with his eyes on the clouds, watching the hawks and
herons that were working up against them, higher
and higher, like so many corkscrews. The truth is,
she was dreadfully alarmed for the prince, who seemed
after a while to lose his head entirely, in the excitement of the chase, and when he got into the open
country he spurred his horse like mad over rocks
and stones, so that she could follow his course by the
trail of sparks which the iron hoofs struck out at
every bound. None of his attendants could keep up
with him but the head huntsman, who had known
him from a child, and who was perfectly devoted to
him; and though both he and his horse were ready to
drop from fatigue, they managed just to keep the
reckless prince in sight.

" Now came the grand catastrophe," said Master

Fleetwood, drawing in his breath, and clenching his hands, while we held our breath in excitement. "Just as the prince was passing a young tree, in whose branches, as it happened, poor Miau-meme was hiding herself, his horse paused suddenly, and a long slender bough struck the poor prince right across both eyes, which were wide open, staring straight up into the sky. He was thrown backward violently to the ground, and his horse, with one rush, crashed into the underbrush, and vanished like a flash of lightning.

"The prince must have felt as if *he* had been struck by lightning, the accident was so— Hurrah! how jolly!" For the attic was suddenly illuminated by a flood of sunshine, and unmistakable blue sky was visible through the small leaded window-panes. Master Fleetwood shuffled his feet impatiently. "Lucky I'm almost done," said he. "Well, the prince wasn't killed, after all; he must have had an awful thick skull; his old falconer had him up in his arms in a twinkling, and he had salts and cologne and things in his pocket to bring him *to*.

I can't stop to go through the particulars, only at last he was leaning his head against a juniper bush as good as new, all but his eyes, — only he had no more strength than a baby, — O, *they* were in a terrible way, all bloodshot, and he could n't open them, and they felt as if a hot poker had been laid across them. A cold wind was blowing right in the prince's face, and it cut his poor eyes like a sharp knife; the poor fellow groaned, and tried to cover them with his hands, but they dropped down limp, he was so weak.

"'Oh! oh! oh!' cried the old falconer, 'I must bind up his poor eyes, or this cold wind will put them out entirely before I can get him home. O dear, dear! your Royal Highness, where is your handkerchief? *where* is your sash?' But the prince's handkerchief had blown away long ago, and he had pulled off his sash and thrown it to a poor half-naked man shaking with rheumatism, who made haste to crouch by the side of the road as the prince whirled past him full gallop, — and the poor falconer could find absolutely *nothing* wherewith he could bind up his dear master's eyes. Of course nobody but princes and such like had handkerchiefs in those days, even the fairies used white rose-petals instead, and the falconer had only one best go-to-church yellow-silk handkerchief, with white spots, and that was safe in his trunk at home. 'O Winastraw,' cried he, after he had looked in vain for something to tie round his master's eyes, 'O cushla ma chree, Savourneen Deelish, och hone, mavourneen, Eileen Ogg, — O, what *shall* I do? This wind will destroy his sight forever.' And while he was wailing and pulling out his gray hair by hands full, what *do* you think the princess was about? She was actually unscrewing her tail, — her beautiful, beloved, adored, precious tail, — that she might offer it to the prince as a bandage for his eyes! You should have heard the cry of joy the old falconer gave, when she thrust it into his hand with one little white paw, while with the other she hid her face, for the tears *would* come into her pretty green eyes after such a dreadful sacrifice as she had made. 'O the soft, warm bandage!' murmured the prince, as the falconer made haste to bind poor Miau-meme's gift over his eyes. 'O, how light, O, how delicate, how comforting! my poor eyes are eased already.' But he was too weak to ask questions, or take much notice; he could not even see poor Miau-meme, who, after all, sacrificed herself to the prince, and never received in return *one* of those soft words, kind looks, or bright smiles that she had so longed for."

Here Master Fleetwood got up, stretched himself, and walked to the door, but he came back to say abruptly, "O, I forgot the point of the story, — the powers above or below, or the fairies, or what you will, took notice of the princess Miau-meme's great sacrifice, and ever since that time the Manx-cats have been tailless, as *she* was all the rest of her life, just in memory of her."

Master Fleetwood went whistling down stairs, three steps at a time, and left us to ponder over the point of the story, as he called it; but we never could decide whether the powers above or the fairies meant to punish or reward poor Miau-meme, by docking the tails of her descendants forever.

VII.

"YOU MUST N'T TOUCH!"

ONE summer my father took country lodgings for his family at a market-gardener's some three miles from town. This gardener not only raised vegetables and flowers, but delicious fruit of all kinds, from early strawberries to late pears. He was always at work in his garden, and he was standing at the gate, spade in hand, when the carriage which brought us from M...... turned into his avenue. We children crowded to the window to look at him, on papa's saying, "There is our landlord." We thought he looked very cross, and no wonder; I suppose he would rather have seen a flock of black-birds settling in his best cherry-tree, than three little girls coming to play all summer in his garden, with their little fingers and thumbs all ready to pick his fruit and flowers. Before mamma had taken her bonnet off in her new lodgings, the poor gardener was knocking at her door, respectfully asking permission " to have a word with the missis." After scratching his head and clearing his throat a good deal, and looking down carefully on the three little heads that hardly reached above his knees, for we little ones came up shyly to make acquaintance with the new landlord, he managed to say that he " thought the young ladies was bigger nor what they was," when he agreed to let his lodgings to " the master." He thought "we was ladies growed,"—a very natural mistake, as very small children are spoken of in England as young ladies and gentlemen, and papa, always in a hurry, had probably not gone into particulars about our ages. Now, seeing that we " was just the wrong size, neither ladies growed, nor hinfants in harms," what was to be done about his garden ? What was to prevent our picking his most valuable flowers and eating his most expensive fruit ? We might be the " ruination" of him, he said, though he tried to put it as politely as possible by repeating, over and over

again, that "children would be children, and very
nateral, ma'am."

"But they need not be *thieves*, Mr. Mason,"
mamma answered austerely, "and I will answer for it
that *my* children sha' n't touch so much as a dan-
delion in your garden without leave." And seeing
him look incredulous, she added, "You may make a
charge on your bill for every currant or gooseberry
they steal, or any flower they steal."

"O ma'am, I should n't go for to call it *stealing*;
just to help theirselves is the nater of little uns,"
said the poor gardener in great confusion, and looking down with a softened eye on little Anne, who, sitting on the carpet, had spied a spot of mud on his
trousers, and was trying to rub it out with her little
forefinger, which she first put into her mouth and
then applied vigorously to the spot with about one-
fly-power.

In short, mamma promised for us that we would
do no mischief in Mr. Mason's garden, that we would
never even pick as much as a green leaf without permission. Perhaps she thought this promise was rather a

rash one, for I remember that she accompanied us on our first walks about the garden, preaching strenuous little sermons to us on the text, "You must n't touch!" And mamma's sermons were effective, for she had no time to impress them upon us by means of reasoning or moral suasion, and if we did not practise what she preached, we got certain little whippings that refreshed our memories wonderfully. Then we had always been accustomed to implicit obedience, and on the whole mamma had little difficulty in training us to respect Mr. Mason's property. Honestly I don't remember a single occasion when we disobeyed her orders "not to touch," and she had reason for the modest pride with which I heard her say to visitors, "My children are pretty good children; on the whole — as children go — they do obey me as well as I can expect."

But the good gardener was delighted; he thought my mother was the most wonderful woman in existence, and that we were the most wonderful children. At first he would follow us about the garden with an anxious face, but when he found he really could depend on our honesty, he began to welcome our coming with pleasure, and soon became very fond of us. He told us one day that he would give us — my sister Anne and myself — little gardens of our own, if we liked, — gardens as big as a pocket-handkerchief. Of course we "liked," and away we ran to find the biggest possible handkerchief as a measure. Little Anne unfolded her precious picture handkerchief, " Poor Richard's Maxims," printed in red, and in rhyme : —

> " For want of a nail the shoe was lost ;
>   For want of a shoe the horse was lost ;
>   For want of a horse the rider was lost."

> " Many strokes fell great oaks."

> " He that by the plough would thrive,
>   Himself must either hold or drive."   Etc., etc.

These were all illustrated with the loveliest deep-red pictures, — a little *blotchy*, to be sure. But this treasure was too small for our purpose. *My* handkerchiefs were made of select pieces cut from the flaps of my father's old linen shirts, and were not only small, but oblong, and we wanted our gardens to be square.

Mrs. Mason, whom we found very busy with her hands in dough, when we ran into the kitchen to ask for *her* handkerchief, told us we might put our hands into her pocket and pull it out for ourselves. We dived deep into the pocket of her stuff petticoat, and pulled out — what looked to be a very snuffy rag, of no particular shape or color. We popped it back again into her pocket, unopened, and, hearing John Cookson, papa's groom, whistling in the yard, we ran out to *him*, clamoring for *his* handkerchief. "'Andkerchaw!" said John, grinning from ear to ear, and showing a splendid set of strong white teeth, " what are you maning, you young uns? Did you ever see *me* with sich a harticle as a 'andkerchaw? *I* don't carry no sich trumpery fallals." And John significantly drew his shirt-sleeve across his nose. Then we ran back to the house and made our request to Mary, who was " redding up" the nursery. She went to the top drawer of the bureau, and produced the desired article in starched cotton, nicely folded, with a blue border and edged with coarse lace, but even with this addition, the handkerchief did not open out as large as one of mamma's made of linen-cambric, which Mary brought us to compare in size with hers. At last we luckily remembered a certain very large yellow bandanna of papa's, too big for his pocket, and which he wore round his neck in cold weather. We told Mr. Mason this, honestly; but he was kind enough to let us take it to measure our gardens by, which made us jump for joy, for it was a full yard square. He marked these gardens off with his spade, side by side; they extended from a peony bush on the right, to a flowering almond on the left, just as the Garden of Eden extended from the Tigris to the Euphrates; and I don't believe the Garden of Eden looked a bit more important to Adam and Eve than our landed property looked to Anna and me, as we stood admiring it, after Mr. Mason had gone off whistling.

Now my genius for landscape-gardening came out in full force; every day my garden was laid out in a new way, and little Anne imitated every change I made. With sharp sticks we drew the walks; sometimes they meandered, sometimes they took the form of a cross or a star. Of course we fenced in our gardens, at first with chips, then with tenpenny **nails,** — rusty, however, for we pulled them out of some **old boards in the cow-shed, and** tore our fingers so badly **that** for a week **Mary** kept **them** bound up in rags. Mrs. Mason one day gave me some old skewers ; she **did it to get** rid of us, for she was perched on the top of a very high step-ladder in the pantry, rummaging the upper shelf, and we probably teased her by walking our dolls, supposed to be angels, up and down the steps, which we called Jacob's ladder. We ran to our gardens with the skewers, **and** made of them some magnificent gateways, interspersed among **the tenpenny nails.** Then we determined to have a chainand-post fence, such as **we had** seen at Denham Park; by dint of long and patient teasing, not only of mamma **and Mary,** but of Betty the cook, Mrs. Mason, and her maid Jane, and even of "old granny" Mason, whom we almost feared to approach because **she** wore an old black-silk hood like a pillow-case **instead** of a cap, we made a collection of darning-needles. These we threaded **upon** two long needlefuls of granny's blue yarn, and set them round our gardens for posts, the yarn which connected them being the chain. Luckily it was *light*, for the posts were few and far between.

At first we made our gardens gay with wild-flowers, and they fairly dazzled our eyes with their splendor when they were stuck full of yellow gorse and dandelions. But as these withered in a day, in spite of all our watering,—and we kept our gardens perfect Sloughs of Despond for their sakes, — we soon got tired of real flowers, and made beautiful ones ourselves from snippings of our sashes and bits of the red flannel that granny used for rheumatism. We thrust pins through our flowers for branches, and then stuck the pins in circles round bits of stick that served us for shrubbery. We worked as hard, in forming elegant groups of this shrubbery, as did the poor gentleman who laid out Studleigh Park, and who regularly climbed to his observatory on the top of a hill, to see the effect of every new tree he planted. Mr. Mason, too, was planting trees,—valuable young fruit-trees, which he protected by little wooden frames, and we too had our slips of plum and cherry trees carefully planted through the centre of empty spools, which we set out in regular rows in what we considered to be the sunniest corner of our gardens.

One day we had two valuable presents, — a Noah's Ark from papa, and a handful of small unsalable radishes from Mr. Mason. Behold us then busy in turning our gardens into wildernesses ; we threw away our ever-flowering shrubbery, even our fruit-trees, and rubbed out our walks with the toes of our shoes. What a trouble it was to lay our gardens down to grass ! We could only carefully put together, like a dissected map, the bits of turf that we were able to scratch up with our little hands, and stamp it down with all the strength of our stout little feet. Then we made a dark forest on one side of our gardens with twigs of juniper, in which the wild beasts of the ark roared and ramped. On the other side, the radishes were planted in squads, like soldiers, and very mar-tial they looked in their red coats, with tufts of tall green feathers in their helmets. Each had a needle stuck through him for a gun, and they were supposed to be defending the settlers on the edge of the wilderness from the wild beasts. These settlers had just come out of the ark, and had set up housekeeping for themselves, in tents made of half egg-shells, over the top of which they gazed fixedly at the lions and tigers.

We enjoyed this tableau so much, that we amused ourselves by inventing others. The grass in our gardens was supposed to be an ocean, in the midst of which floated the ark; by that time it had fortunately lost its cover, so that Mmes. Shem, Ham, and Japhet could conveniently look down from the top and admire the bravery of their husbands, boldly navigating the ark by means of slate-pencils (oars) on the deck below. The radishes and the wild beasts lay scattered about on their sides, drowned, and the dove and the raven were hopefully in view, astride over a couple of tree-tops in the forest. Another time we turned Noah into Christopher Columbus; we had to nail him with a tack to the top of the ark, now a Spanish galleon, as we found it difficult to keep his face turned toward the New World, — the juniper forest, wherein the resuscitated radishes figured as red Indians, with feathers on their heads.

Our gardens were everything by turns, and nothing long. We had a boarding-school there for our dolls; we came there as travellers ourselves. Our gardens bore in turn the names of all the countries of Europe that we could spell out on the map. If they were Turkey, we gobbled, gobbled, to each other by way of speaking the language; if Switzerland, we made a hissing with our mouths that sounded like *Swiss, Swiss*; if France, we repeated over and over, *We, we, we ;* if Hungary, we made a sound of *chewing* with our jaws. In giving us those small squares of ground, good Mr. Mason had done the best possible thing for his own garden as far as *we* were concerned ; we were so absorbed in them that we forgot everything else. The gardener and his men were busy at work all about us every day : they picked fruit for market, and gathered flowers for what they called " cottage-bouquets," because they were composed of simple garden-flowers ; but we took no notice of them. I remember the " red-haired currant-bushes," as we called them, thickly covered with clusters of fruit, hanging like short curls, and the brown rows of jargonelle pears suspended from slender branches trained along the garden walls, like the bells in the coffee-room of the " Manchester Arms." You see, objects were doubly interesting to me, because they always put me in mind of something different from themselves. And I remember seeing tall Mr. Mason in the greenhouse, with my little sister Lucretia perched, light as a butterfly, on his shoulder. From this elevation she would peep at us through the vine-branches trained along the low glass roof, her clean pinafore gleaming white among the leaves, and the vine-tendrils clustering about her face, and twisting themselves round her own short curls.

Now it so happened that Mr. Mason possessed an apple-tree of so rare and peculiar a kind that he had thought it worthy of a conspicuous place in his garden, and he had therefore set it out in the little grass-plot, right in front of the house, and in full view of the windows. This tree was young, and was bearing this summer for the first time. It was ornamented with a few clusters of pink and white blossoms, when we first took possession of our lodgings, and we soon learned to feel a great sympathy with Mr. Mason when we saw him walking about the little tree, with his hands in his pockets and his pipe in his mouth, wondering what sort of apples would grow in place of those blossoms, whose white petals would drift slowly down upon his nose when he stopped to survey them. After they were all blown away, half a dozen little green knobs appeared in their places. We passed the tree often on our way to and from the house, and when we saw Mr. Mason standing under it, scrutinizing those little knobs, we used to run and take him by the hand and stare up at them too, wrinkling the tops of our little noses, and shading our eyes from the sun, just as he did. He watched those baby apples, so we thought, as closely as mamma watched our baby, and when a tinge of red appeared in their cheeks, he showed as much pleasure as mamma did when our poor pale baby began to get a little color. We listened respectfully when Mr. Mason read to us the name of the tree, which was printed in Latin on a slip

239

of wood and tied to a convenient bough, and we wondered, in sympathy with him, what its fruit would be like when it was ripe. Little Anne only hoped it would be " *nice*," while *I* pictured the apples to myself as gorgeously beautiful as new red morocco balls with orange stripes.

Well, the days and the weeks of that beautiful summer slipped away, and the different fruits in Mr. Mason's garden ripened, came to perfection, and passed away in turn; mamma was an excellent customer, buying as much of it for us as she thought we ought to eat. Cherries, strawberries, currants, raspberries, how beautiful they looked, red and white, heaped up in mamma's cut-glass bowls! yet we thought no fruit in the garden half as handsome as the apples ripening on the little tree in the middle of the grass-plot. They turned out to be summer apples of the largest size, swelling out suddenly in the July heat, almost as rapidly as soap-bubbles, into great globes of color, really not so much unlike our morocco balls, after all! And one day, after smelling at them as carefully as if they were so many nosegays,

240

and pinching them very gently with his thumb and finger, Mr. Mason pronounced them to be ripe, and declared he should soon pick them.

Now it happened that the largest, reddest, roundest, yellowest apple of all hung nearly within our reach, at the end of a long slender branch that had been growing downwards all summer under its weight. When my sister Anne saw Mr. Mason examining the fruit on the little tree, she wished to touch this apple for herself, that she might see whether it was ripe; she thought Mr. Mason would value *her* opinion on the subject. So, with great labor, I held her up, wavering in the air, while she laid her small finger solemnly on the rosy apple, bobbing above her head. As soon as she found herself safe on the ground again, she ran to Mr. Mason and pronounced *her* verdict, — "*yipe!* no, I mean *wipe*," for she was often corrected for her manner of pronouncing the letter *R.* "Ah! ah! ah! (R!)" said the gardener, shaking his finger at her playfully, though I don't think she appreciated the pun, "but you should n't touch, you know, — must n't touch the apple again." "No, in-

deed," cried Mary, hurrying up to see what we were
about, — "no, Miss Anne, you must n't touch."
Mamma now appeared at the parlor window, and,
seeing us all together on the grass-plot, she was, as
usual, afraid that something was wrong. "What's
the matter, Mary?" cried she; "have the children
done anything naughty?" She was apt to think that
we either *had been* naughty, *were* naughty, or were
going to be naughty. "No, ma'am," said Mary, in
her shrill treble, "I was only telling Miss Anne she
must n't touch." "No, no, children, don't touch, be
sure you don't touch!" said mamma, speaking on
general principles.

I dare say you think Mr. Mason was very stingy
about his apples, but the truth was, he meant to send
them to a horticultural show in M......, as they were
of a new and rare variety. Now, when he went to
gather them, he found to his surprise the very apple
on which little Anne had laid her finger, the handsomest of the half-dozen that grew on the tree, still
hanging from the end of the branch, but with a piece
bitten out of one side. Mr. Mason took it into the

house and showed my mother the marks of little teeth upon it. Mamma was very much concerned. "Little Eve has bitten the apple," the gardener said, laughing ; in fact he laughed and chuckled to himself about it so much that mamma could not understand it, yet she was very glad that he did not seem as vexed and sorry as she had expected, for she knew the value he set on his rare fruit.

"But which of the children did it?" asked she. "I must punish the little thing severely, and I am more grieved than I can tell, to think that one of my children should have been so very, very naughty."

"Now, missus," said the gardener, still laughing, "don't take it to heart, there was nothing naughty about it. I won't tell you who did it, unless you promise me you won't punish the little *gal*."

"You are very kind to make light of the matter," said mamma, gravely, "but the little girl who bit your apple did a very wicked thing, and I can't promise to overlook it."

Just then we came running into the room, Anne and I, freshly dressed, washed, and curled for the afternoon by careful Mary, and we both spied at once the bitten apple in Mr. Mason's hand.

"Little girls who steal will also tell lies, I know," said mamma, taking each of us by the hand and making us stand in front of her, so that she could study our faces. We looked up wonderingly, and we caught the reflection of ourselves, two little fairies in white, peeping at us out of mamma's beautiful brown eyes, which were bent on us with severity. But I am sure she saw no guilt in our two astonished faces. "Do you see the apple in Mr. Mason's hand?" said mamma, sternly. "One of you little girls bit that piece out of it; I hope you won't add to your fault by telling a lie about it." And she looked first at me and then at Anne, baffled by our apparent innocence. "*Which* of you bit that apple?"

"O, *I* did," answered little Anne simply, as if relieved at having a question she could understand. "I did it yesterday afternoon just before tea. I don't want to tell a lie, mamma. I took the little black footstool, and I could reach the apple beautifully, and I bit out as big a piece as I could, and it tasted ever so nice." And she continued to look in mamma's face as if she could not get over her surprise at seeing it so sober.

Mamma was equally surprised at Anne's manner and way of speaking; the dear child showed no sense of guilt or shame.

"Don't you know that you have been a very naughty, disobedient girl?" said she. "Don't you remember how often I have told you not to touch those apples, — over and over again?"

"O, but, mamma," cried Anne, eagerly, as if a new light had broken in upon her, "did you really think I touched? Are you angry because you thought I touched? Well, I *did n't* touch, I *did* remember what you said. When I stood on the footstool, I just clasped my hands together behind my back, so that I should be *sure* not to touch, and I held 'em so all the time, — though it *did* make me tumble off the stool." And she showed a black and blue spot on her soft white arm, and looked up into mamma's face with the most innocent eyes in the world.

"It's just so, missus, just as she tells it," said Mr.

Mason, coming forward. "I seen her do it. I seen her bite the apple in the cutest way, with her two little hands at the back of her pinafore. She did n't go for to do one mite of wrong, I do assure you; and it was seein' her a-tiptoe atop of that stool! and herself patiently trying to stick her teeth in the apple, which knocked against her little nose like a pendulum a-swinging,—I say it was *that* made me laugh so, missus, just now, a-thinking of it, and you must not scold her a bit." And Mr. Mason laughed again as he drew this little picture.

Anne laughed too. "O mamma," said she, "I was *so* afraid of knocking the apple off, when it bobbed about so. Because if I *had*, if it *had* tumbled on the ground, I should not have got one single taste of it,—for you know you told us we must n't touch, so I *could n't* have picked it up."

We were still standing at mamma's knee, and as she looked down into Anne's eager little face, I noticed that the tiny fairies in her eyes seemed to be suddenly caught in a shower. There were certainly drops of water in mamma's eyes, but I never suspected they were *tears,* or that grown-up people ever cried. Why, even children never cried for *nothing,* and nobody had been scolding mamma, or telling *her* " not to touch." I saw her stoop, and kiss tenderly the black and blue spot on Anne's little round arm, without finding any fault with the dear child, after all ; and then I suppose she went quietly away, for I only remember as the conclusion of the matter, a certain delightful journey on horseback that my sister and I performed sitting one on each of Mr. Mason's corduroy knees. On these hard trotting horses we made several journeys to London and back again with such speed as almost to take away our breath, and we should have tumbled off our slippery side-saddle, if Mr. Mason had not held us firmly in his strong arms.

There was a delightful moment on every return trip from London, when we met at full gallop, like knights in a tournament, and when Mr. Mason did his best to knock our heads together, as we passed each other. We resisted with might and main, and there was plenty of screaming and laughing and prancing of fiery steeds. Horses and riders were glad to rest at last, and partake of refreshments in the shape of the bitten apple, which Mr. Mason generously cut up into mouthfuls with his jack-knife, and divided between us, taking a bite himself, once in a while, by way of toll.

248

THE END.

Printed at the University Press, Cambridge.